Dedication

To my kids, Mike, Brandy, Christy, and Nick, thanks for all the support and great ideas. I'm so blessed to have you. And for all the horse lovers I've known throughout the years. This book is for you.

Racing For Love
Night Life – Book Two

Dani Petrone

Print ISBNs
Amazon print 9780228629283
Ingram Spark 9780228629290
BWL Print

Table of Contents

Chapter One

The radio in Colton McKenna's beat-up pickup blasted a catchy country tune that echoed through the air as he rolled into the backside parking lot of the Sonoran Turf racetrack. Glancing at his watch, he grimaced. Five-fifty-five. The morning seemed to have sprouted wings and flew away from him. Colton preferred to get started long before daylight.

He offered a causal wave to the security guard and, as the gate lifted, drove straight to his favorite spot, strategically close to the track's backside kitchen. Once parked, Colton grabbed *The Daily Racing Form* from the passenger seat, jumped out, and headed toward barn number 12—time to get to work.

Blades of grass in the lawn area, still damp from an overnight sprinkle of rain, glistened in the bright morning sunlight. The sweet smell of hay and the pungent odor of fresh manure assaulted his nostrils. Some folks hated those smells, but nothing was more comforting to Colton. As a horse whinnied in the distance, he inhaled deeply and smiled. Yeah, this was where he belonged.

He also appreciated these Arizona January mornings. Cool and crisp, but Colton expected he'd be sweating up a storm and shedding layers of clothing by noon. The weather forecast was singing to the tune of the high sixties with a clear sky. Perfect racing weather once that blazing ball of fire took center stage.

"Morning, McKenna."

Recognizing the man's voice, Colton halted and turned toward the source. James Ledger, Thoroughbred horse breeder and the owner of the notorious Tribal Jack. Ledger was like a fox, always one step ahead and probably the only owner who considered this early to be a good time to show up at the sheds. Usually, all Colton ran into before ten A.M. were the backside workers, exercise riders, grooms, jockeys looking for their next ride, and the trainers.

A nod acknowledged Ledger's presence, followed by a casual, "Morning."

The man's narrow lips stretched into a sly smile, revealing the hint of something devious lurking beneath the surface. "Sorry about Thompson," he said, the words dripping with feigned empathy. "You know, if you're ever looking for a change of pace, my stable is always open for someone like you."

Colton's jaw tightened momentarily. "Thanks," He offered. Yeah, like hell he'd work for James Ledger. Everyone working on the backside knew the man's shady reputation. It hung on him like a dark cloud. Sure, Ledger's offer had the allure of fame and fortune, but the moral compass of Colton's principles wasn't easily swayed. He responded politely but firmly. "Appreciate the offer, but I'm doing fine."

Ledger pulled a pair of designer sunglasses from his front shirt pocket. He blew dust from them, his expression narrowing and eyes gleaming with a predatory glint before slipping them onto his face.

Colton's intuition sparked a silent alarm. The casual puff of invisible dust and the calculated sunglasses slide were more than gestures. They were signals, a sly dance.

The transition was seamless, Ledger's voice dripping with a touch of venom hidden under layers of veneer. "So, what's the news with Icy Tears? Met the new owner yet?"

"Not yet."

"When you do, let them know I'll pay a good price for him."

"Sure. I'll pass the information along." Colton nodded, then continued walking toward the barn. He had no plans to stand around and chit-chat. The man grated on his nerves. It was like Ledger's words carried an evil intention that he figured you were too naive to realize. Colton wasn't.

Colton stepped into the tack room he used for his office, tossed *The Daily Racing*

Form onto his old, battered desk, and headed straight for the coffee pot. Once he hit the start button, he planted himself in his chair, opened the paper, and started scribbling notes next to a jockey or a horse's name.

"Who ya got for me this morning?"

Colton swung around in his chair and smiled at the girl standing in the doorway. He knew Bree, the twenty-year-old exercise rider, was being a smart ass. His string of horses, by today's count, was three. If the new owner of his best one sold him, his number would be two. And of those remaining two, one had a bad leg. Colton ran his hand through his hair. He needed a new client with a decent horse to hire him...quickly. His feed bills, payroll, vet visits, and personal living expenses were stacking up.

Colton scratched his chin. "Take Icy Tears out first."

"You got it." Bree walked to the whiteboard and put a bold check mark next to the name Icy Tears. "He's showing promise. I think he is my favorite."

"Yeah. Well, don't get too attached. I don't know what the new owner has in mind." Colton rose from his chair and reached for a mug on the shelf above the coffee stand. As he poured the steaming brew into the cup, he added, "Tell José I'll want to check the filly's leg shortly."

"Will do." Bree picked up her gear and headed out the doorway.

Colton took a swig of coffee, grimaced at the taste, then set the cup on his desk. If he weren't running so damn late this morning, he would have had time to grab a decent cup from the track's kitchen. He turned and snatched his well-worn baseball cap from the hook near the doorway, shoved it on, and stepped outside.

I better check the horses. At least while I still have some to work with.

As Colton walked toward Icy Tears, two horses poked their heads out of the stalls. "Morning, girls," he muttered to them in passing.

He reached the third stall and stepped inside the small enclosure where José was helping Bree adjust the saddle. The dark bay snorted restlessly and stamped his foreleg. Large eyes full of spirit watched Colton anxiously.

While running his hand along the muscled shoulder, he calmly spoke, "Hey there, big guy."

Icy Tears bobbed his head as Colton stepped back and observed José. The groom had already mucked the stall, brushed him down, cleaned all four feet, wrapped his legs, and now assisted Bree.

José glanced toward Colton. "He's looking good this morning."

"We'll see how good he looks after his workout." Colton stepped aside as Bree led her mount out of the enclosure. "Billy Ray's your pony guy today, and he should be waiting for you."

"Yep. I just texted him that I'm on my way."

Colton gave her a leg up into the saddle.

Once mounted, she buckled her helmet and picked up the reins. "There he comes now. See you soon." She gave him a wave as she headed off to meet Billy Ray.

Colton watched as Bree, now guided by Billy Ray, moved along the horse path toward the training track. He took a deep breath and scratched the back of his neck while observing the two riders. He planned to clock Icy Tears workout as soon as he checked on the filly.

Reaching Ardent Moment's stall, he carefully walked inside. José had the grey's leg in the soaking boot filled with ice water. Colton ran his hand along her shoulder. She lowered her head to rub against his back several times before turning to grab a mouthful of hay from the hay net.

José entered. "Leg's looking better. Maybe work her out soon?"

"Vet's coming this morning. Fingers crossed."

The groom nodded and smiled.

"Excuse me." A female called from nearby.

Colton turned toward the sound of a voice he didn't recognize. "I'm looking for Colton McKenna?"

Wondering who could be looking for him, Colton excused himself from José's questioning gaze and stepped from the stall. He found himself staring into the face of a beautiful woman.

"I'm Colton McKenna." He pushed back his baseball cap and then wiped his palms along the sides of his jeans. "How can I help you?"

"Trisha Thompson." She extended her hand toward him. "I'm the new owner of Icy Tears. I believe it's you I need to speak with?"

Colton's eyebrows lifted as he flashed her a smile. "Nice to meet *you*, Miss Thompson."

His day just took a turn he wasn't expecting. It had been his understanding that Bobby Thompson's daughter wouldn't be around for another week. *Damn shame. Bobby was too young for a heart attack. But then, age doesn't play a part when your time is up.*

The brunette took his hand and gave it a firm shake. Colton stared at the woman now standing before him. He hadn't thought about what Thompson's daughter might look like. The only picture of her he'd ever seen was of a three-year-old little girl, and this was no little girl.

She pulled her hand from his. "Please, call me Trisha."

Colton motioned toward the tack room. "Let's head inside and talk, Trisha." Noticing a clump of manure one of the horses had left outside the stall, he took her arm. "Watch your step."

"Thank you." She sidestepped slightly so her high-heeled boots would avoid the mess.

Colton fell in step behind her as they headed toward the tack room that served as his office. He suspected she didn't notice how his gaze moved to her backside. The way that short skirt hugged her curvy hips would tempt any man. And Colton was a man who enjoyed a curvy woman.

Once inside, Colton pulled a chair from the side of his desk and gestured for her to sit. He sat while waiting for her to settle and began sizing her up. She was in her late twenties, probably about five-foot-five. Hard to tell wearing those spike heels. Nicely shaped face, big eyes, long dark hair, curvy in just the right places.

He cleared his throat. "Would you like coffee? I can brew a fresh pot. I wasn't expecting you today, or I'd have brought some cookies."

She didn't answer.

He cleared his throat again, suddenly embarrassed by his rambling. "Bottled water? There's some in the fridge over there."

"No, thank you."

He offered her a smile. "If you change your mind, feel free to help yourself."

Manicured fingers that didn't look like they'd ever shoveled manure held up some paperwork. "Here, Mr. McKenna. The new contract for you to continue as a trainer for Icy Tears." She placed several papers secured together with a paperclip on his desk.

Colton glanced down at the paperwork and then back to the woman sitting beside him. He caught a whiff of her perfume. Sweet and agreeable, something like a vanilla sugar cookie. He picked the contract up.

"You'll find everything in order. My attorney wrote it up for me."

"Your attorney?"

"Yes. My friend, Rebecca Harris, took care of everything."

"Did she? Including getting your Department of Racing license?"

"Yes. I've checked with the secretary's office. Everything is in order. Do you need to see a copy?"

"Maybe later." Colton glanced over the first page of the paperwork. "You do realize what I charge?"

"I plan to discuss that with you today. I'm sure we can work something out."

"Work out?" Colton rocked back slightly in his chair. "I don't work payment out. My rate for you is one hundred dollars a day. That's what your daddy paid me, and it'll be the same for you." He scratched his chin, then continued. "You'll be responsible for handling anything over the regular veterinary costs on your own."

She tensed and then leaned forward slightly. "My father left me enough funds to get started, Mr. McKenna. I expect you to get the horse into the correct races so he'll earn enough to pay your fees and build up my bank account."

Colton opened his mouth to comment, then clamped his lips together, thinking it better to remain silent.

"So, sign the contract, and we'll be off to the races as they say." She stood, hiked her handbag strap onto the shoulder, and, with a tilt of her head, gave him a smile.

Colton frowned. "You own a horse before?"

"No."

He nodded. "You ever ridden before?"

"Of course, I've ridden a horse." She narrowed her gaze and placed her hands on both her hips.

Colton bit back a groan. He nodded again as his eyes traveled from her mid-thigh skirt down her long legs to the tips of her high-heeled boots. He smiled tightly.

"My friend took me riding one summer." She shrugged, then, meeting his stare, added proudly, "I was a teenager, but she taught me a lot about horses."

"I'm sure she did," Colton mumbled under his breath. He picked the contract up and glanced at it again. "I need to give this working arrangement some thought."

Damn, this girl has no clue what she's getting into here. And *right* now, he wasn't sure if he wanted to get involved. There was a good possibility she'd lose her money, and no matter how hard he worked to keep that from happening, there was no guarantee in horseracing. After all, it was called gambling.

Ignoring his remark, she asked, "When may I see my horse?" Her eyebrows lifted.

Colton dropped the paperwork back on his desk. "Exercise girl should be bringing him back anytime." *I should have been out there watching his workout.* Colton stood and motioned toward the door. "After you."

Colton ushered Trisha out of the tack room. They entered the bright morning as Bree rode up on Icy Tears. On his exercise pony, Billy Ray guided them toward the hotwalker area where José waited. Once José took the reins, Bree jumped from the saddle, quickly removed her helmet, and wiped her sweaty brow. "He did great this morning."

Colton nodded. "Sorry I missed it. Write me up a report and leave it on my desk."

"Absolutely. I'm taking Queenie out if she's ready."

"She's ready," José told her as he removed the saddle. Then he replaced the bridle with a halter and shank. He headed to the washstand and began spraying him down. After he'd wiped Icy Tears dry, he hooked him to the hotwalker, then headed for the stall to assist Bree.

"What do you think of your horse?" Colton asked Trisha as he pointed toward her horse.

"Oh, he's beautiful." She squinted in the sunlight. "And so big."

"Yeah, he's a big one, all right. Seventeen hands, and sound as a dollar. Your daddy had an eye for horseflesh."

She didn't answer, only took a step forward. As she did, Colton noticed her high heels sink into the soft grass and mud caused by water runoff from the washstand, and she seemed unaware.

"May I pet him?" Excitement tinged her voice.

"I'd wait until he's back in his stall. He's still a little worked up from his exercise. Let him cool down, and we'll get him inside, and you can give him a carrot."

Trisha frowned and tucked a lock of dark hair that had blown across her face behind her ear. "A carrot? Let me remind you, McKenna, I own this horse."

Colton blinked, surprised by her outburst.

She planted both hands on her hips. "I'll pet or feed him anytime I want, and I don't need your permission." She stepped backward to free her boot from the mud while swinging her handbag over her shoulder.

"Watch it!" Colton hollered, too late.

Trisha had misjudged the distance between herself and the horse. The movement startled Icy Tears, causing him to jerk his head on the hotwalker. Still high on adrenaline from his workout, he lunged and cow-kicked outward, his back leg barely missing Trisha.

Trisha screamed, sending Icy Tears into another fit. The horse reared and lunged again, ears pinned and mouth open.

Colton grabbed her and yanked hard, but not before Icy Tears sank his teeth into the handbag she'd slung over her shoulder. She was still screaming as they hit the ground together and rolled. When they stopped moving, Colton lay on his back in the mud with Trisha on top, pressed tightly against his chest. Their eyes locked. Colton scowled, letting her know he wasn't happy.

By now, every horse in the shedrow was making a fuss.

José and Bree came running. Bree immediately turned the hotwalker off while José, moving to the inside, grabbed the halter. A few seconds passed before José calmed him down, got him off the walker, and led him toward his stall.

"Are you okay?" Colton couldn't decide if he wanted to hug her or shake her. The woman had scared the bejabbers out of him, not to mention the horse could have seriously hurt her.

This is why you don't let just anyone in the backside area. Too much can happen; injure themselves or mess up a horse.

Colton got to his feet, dragging Trisha with him. "Don't you know better than to spook a horse? Miss, I-know-all-about-horses, Thompson. You could have been hurt."

They stared at each other for a moment before either spoke. Trisha was trembling and trying to catch her breath. She pulled away from him and attempted to brush off the mud on her skirt. Finally, she gazed up at him. "It won't happen again. I promise."

Colton wasn't sure he believed her. He looked into her big brown eyes and saw nothing but trouble. If he had a lick of sense, he'd tell her to leave and send him an address to have her horse delivered. Away from his barn and away from him. Colton blew out a breath.

"Thank you for saving me." She blinked her thick eyelashes. A sudden breeze blew through and lifted her dark waves off her shoulders. She shivered.

A grain of guilt pricked his conscience for yelling at her. "Come on in the tack room and warm up."

"No. I'd rather go home and change." She pulled her jacket tighter to her body, then added in a softer voice, "Thanks for the offer, though."

"Okay." He bent, picked up his cap from the ground, and slapped it against his leg to shake off the dirt.

"I'll be back tomorrow. I want to watch Icy Tears workout." Then she added with a sarcastic tone, "If it's agreeable with you, Mr. McKenna."

Rolling his eyes, Colton sighed, then trying to keep his voice firm answered, "Be here in the morning by six." Without waiting for her response, he headed to the tack room, stopped, turned, and hollered. "Hey. Wear some better shoes. And call me Colton."

"Yes, sir." She saluted him then added, "See you tomorrow, Colton."

Watching her walk away, he couldn't help but smile as he noticed the cute little wiggle of her hips. Still grinning, Colton stepped inside the room he used as his office and glanced at the clock on the wall. A veterinarian would arrive soon to do another x-ray on the filly's leg. He slid into his chair and reached across his desk for Trisha's contract, snatched it up, and read through it, studying each word.

Releasing a groan, Colton picked up a pen.

Chapter Two

What a difference a few days make. Trisha stared at the margarita in her hand and blew out a breath. She'd heard people say those words many times before but never really thought about the meaning...until now.

Last month, she had no complications. She had a great job in a busy public relations office. She'd saved enough money to buy a condo in a lovely, quiet neighborhood. She was single, happy, and stress-free. Then her father, a man, by his absence, she'd assumed didn't give a hoot about her, died, leaving her all his worldly possessions. In the blink of an eye, Trisha owned a racehorse and sixty acres in northern Arizona.

She glanced at her two best friends sitting across the table, Scarlett and Rayna. They'd met at this upscale bar and grill near central Phoenix called the Ritz for a happy hour almost every Thursday since college. The Ritz was the local hangout for white-collar professionals. Until a few months ago, there had been four of them getting together for cocktails. Only now, Rebecca was married, and tonight, she was with her husband. That was okay with Trisha; she completely understood. Her friends' lives were changing, too.

"So, tell us what happened when you met with the horse trainer," Scarlett asked.

Scarlett wore her winter signature look, a black skirt and white sweater. Her auburn hair was freshly curled, floating down her back in perfect waves. Oversized silver hoop earrings studded with crystals sparkled against her creamy complexion, and a sprinkle of glitter dusted her cheekbones.

"Yes. I can't wait to hear how that went," Rayna added. Her short platinum curls, tipped in pink, swished around her neck as she spoke. She straightened, her tight stretch top hugging her delicate curves. "Spill it."

A wistful smile tugged at Trisha's lips, and she leaned forward, "He's the most beautiful thing I've ever seen."

"The trainer guy?" Scarlett asked, eyes wide.

"No. Sorry, I was deep in thought. I meant my horse. My horse is beautiful."

"What about the trainer? We want to hear what he's like?" Rayna insisted.

Trisha rolled her eyes. "Fine." She leaned in and met her friend's curious stares. "He's arrogant and bossy. He's, oh, I don't know how to describe him."

"Start by telling us he's hot," Rayna stated.

Trisha shrugged. "I guess he's hot. I didn't notice." She calmly stirred her margarita with the swizzle stick.

"She didn't notice." Scarlett and Rayna spoke in unison while struggling not to laugh.

Frowning, Trisha leaned forward. "Look, you two. I've had a miserable day. I went to the racetrack before breakfast, got attacked by a horse, and then rolled in freezing mud with the trainer. Oh, and the horse took a bite of my three-hundred-dollar handbag." She held up her purse and pointed to the teeth marks.

"Holy crap." Scarlett's eyes widened.

Rayna straightened in her chair and gasped. "Good Heavens."

Trisha tossed the handbag onto the seat beside her. "Then I had to rush home and get cleaned up so I wouldn't be late for my work luncheon meeting. At which the client had the nerve to tell me he didn't like my suggestions for his company logo." She took a drink from her margarita glass. "After that, I rushed home to change clothes again to meet you two, and my hair wouldn't cooperate." She ran her fingers through the loose strands hanging along her cheek. "That's why I have this messy bun look." She blew out a long breath. "What I need now is another margarita."

"I need to hear more about rolling around in the mud with the trainer." Scarlett tilted her head and wiggled her eyebrows.

"Seriously. That's what you heard in all that?" Trisha's nerves were frayed, and she'd come to the Ritz to relax, not to deal with teasing.

"It's what I heard," Rayna added.

"Well, you'll have to wait another day to hear the story. Tonight, I don't want to talk about Colton McKenna."

Trisha glanced around the crowded room. Everywhere she looked, handsome men in crisp dress shirts mingled and laughed with young women dressed in skirts and fancy blouses. Not a pair of well-worn jeans or a baseball cap in sight. Young professionals, what she'd always wanted to be a part of...until now. Over the last few days since learning of her father's will, her mind had wandered to rugged men in tight, faded jeans and solid, muscled arms who worked hard outside, not just exercised in a gym. Immediately, Colton entered her mind. She had to admit he *was* hot. Startled by her thoughts, she blinked, picked up her drink, and drained the glass.

"Are you okay?" Scarlett asked.

"Yeah. Why?"

"You seemed to have drifted off for a minute." Scarlett raised her eyebrows.

"Oh, I'm just tired." She sighed. "It's been a long day."

"Totally understand." Changing the subject, Scarlett said, "Hey, are you hungry?"

"I'm starving," Rayna answered. "Let's order something."

"I'll take mine home if you don't mind." Trisha offered a weak smile. "Sorry, but I'm exhausted."

"What about this weekend?" Scarlett asked. "I'm thinking of Lazy Jake's. They have a new band playing, and something else is happening there, too. I'll check their website."

"I think there's a dance contest. Anyway, I'm down for a good-looking guy in a cowboy hat." Rayna turned to Trisha, "You in?"

"Sure." Trisha shrugged. "Why not? Sounds like fun."

"Great." Rayna answered, then quickly added, "Let's order some food."

Later that evening, after changing into her pajamas, Trisha settled herself in front of the television. She'd poured a glass of red zinfandel to accompany her steak salad with roasted broccoli and baby carrots. As she ate, she channel-surfed, looking for something interesting.

She stopped at a romantic comedy. The handsome hero who filled the screen had caught her attention. He was tall and looked like he'd been on horseback herding cattle all day. *This looks interesting. A rough-and-tumble cowboy romance could be entertaining.* She took a sip of wine and leaned back slightly.

The cowboy strode purposely from the barn toward the fence railing with a confident swagger. The camera zoomed in closer. Thick brown hair and a day's worth of stubble covered his strong jaw. This guy reminded her of someone. Names of actors raced through her mind. Then recognition hit. The actor in this movie reminded her of Colton. Straightening, Trisha grabbed the remote and changed the channel.

Chapter Three

Trisha was wide awake the following morning fifteen minutes before her alarm went off. This surprised her because she usually hit the snooze button several times before fully opening her eyes.

With no in-person appointments scheduled at her job, it didn't take her long to shower and dress. She could get away with casual attire, so she decided on jeans, a sweater, and, most importantly, a pair of sneakers instead of her usual high heels. Now, all she needed was a good jolt of caffeine.

Forty-five minutes later, Trisha drove past the guard gate at the racetrack and pulled into a spot near the backside kitchen. Opening her car door, she was immediately hit by the smell of fried potatoes, bacon, onions, and coffee. The smells reminded her of the cafe she'd worked at during college. Those hours had been long and exhausting but worth it. She'd graduated with a bachelor's degree in business, which would be helpful now that she was a valid business owner.

A feeling of pride rushed through her as the reality of that thought hit. She was a small business owner. It was a horse racing business, something that had never entered her mind when considering her options. Nevertheless, it was all hers. Now, all she needed was a company name, and she'd be up and rolling, and that detail was on her list for this afternoon. Feeling optimistic about her future, Trisha hiked her handbag on her shoulder and headed for Colton McKenna's barn.

Trisha glanced into the tack room and found no one inside. However, she did notice a coffee cup and an open race form on his desk. *Colton must be here somewhere.*

She left the tack room, hoping to find him as José appeared from the second stall, leading the grey horse.

"Morning. Is Colton around?"

José motioned for her to step closer to the wall as he answered, "She kicks."

Realizing he wanted to pass without worrying about her being kicked, she did as he instructed.

"Mr. McKenna's out there." He pointed toward the workout track.

Trisha nodded. "Thank you." She watched José lead the horse into the open area. Trisha pushed a stray strand of hair from her face and headed toward the track.

The morning was chilly, but the weather prediction for the day said it would get into the sixties. Trisha shoved her hands into her jacket pockets and took a deep breath. The air carried in a distinct smell of horses. Manure, dirt, freshly mowed grass, strong coffee, and the lingering aroma of fried bacon and eggs from the backside kitchen filled her with surprisingly good aromas. It amazed her how much she enjoyed being here.

She reached the workout track and, glancing around, didn't see Colton anywhere. She leaned against the railing as a horse galloped into view, followed by two more horses and riders.

Trisha found herself mesmerized. Powerful animals, their muscles straining, coats gleaming in the early morning sunshine, steam blowing from nostrils, hooves pounding the ground.

She could see how easily one got caught up in the excitement of crossing the finish line first. *This must be the dream of every horseman, to be number one. The excitement, the hope, the prestige, and, of course, the gamble.*

"Well, look who's here bright and early."

Startled from being deep in thought, Trisha turned and couldn't help but notice how handsome he looked in the bright sunlight. She gave him a warm smile. "Good morning."

His eyes met hers. Colton moved beside her and rested his arms on the top rail, placing his boot over the lowest. He pointed toward the approaching rider, "Here comes your horse."

Trisha excitedly turned her attention toward the track and smiled. Icy Tears moved closer, tossing his head, snorting, his muscles quivering beneath his dark bay coat. His hooves danced in the dirt as Bree tried to hold him in place.

"Let's see what he's got this morning," Bree told Colton as she guided her mount closer to the rail. Then, noticing Trisha, she added, "Nice to see you again."

"You too," Trisha answered as Bree turned the horse's nose toward the middle of the racetrack and pressed her knees into his sides.

As Trisha watched Icy Tears break into a gallop, a sudden rush of emotion overcame her. *I wonder if this is how my dad felt—watching his horse work out—anticipating the thrill of a future win.*

"Uh, oh, lady. I've seen that look before."

Trisha glanced at Colton. "What look?"

A smile creased the corners of his mouth. "The one a horseman gets while watching his Thoroughbred on the track. Your daddy got that look, and I see it in your eyes, too."

Trisha's stomach tightened as he scrutinized her. "You see a woman excited to start her new business."

He nodded, and his smile seemed amused. "Maybe. But it's more than a business pumping your blood. It's the thrill of the win." His eyes narrowed as he observed her closely. Too close. "Yep, same look as your daddy."

Sending him a 'you're wrong' glare, she shrugged. *This man knows more about my father than I do. Or ever will.* Still, it was hard to argue with his words. Trisha did feel an excitement she couldn't explain. A quickening in her heart as she watched the horses.

She shrugged. "They are magnificent, and I admit it's hard not to get excited."

Colton nodded. His blue eyes glinted, and the corners of his lips lifted. "Don't worry, Boss Lady, your secret is safe with me."

"Thank you for acknowledging me as your employer. However, you haven't uncovered any secrets about me."

Colton laughed and lifted one eyebrow as if he sensed a dare. "Nothing prettier than watching a Thoroughbred do what they're bred to do. Especially with a lovely woman."

Her heart did a silly little thump. She licked her lips nervously, and Colton's gaze skated to her mouth before returning to her eyes. She shook her head slowly and told him, "Watch the horses."

Colton laughed again.

They stood quietly for the next ten minutes, observing the riders as they galloped past, Colton making barely audible comments now and again to himself. The wind picked up, her hair lifted in the breeze, and strands blew across her face. Trisha smoothed them back and shivered. She should have worn a heavier jacket this morning but thought it would be warm enough when the sun came out.

"You want a cup of coffee?" Colton asked.

"Yes, please."

"Come on. I'm buying."

Together, they headed toward the track's kitchen. They passed a few men along the way. Each greeted Colton and asked if he had anything running. Colton's cheerful answer was the same for everyone. "Nothing in today's lineup."

They reached the kitchen, and Colton held the door open for her. Inside was about what she'd expected. It was nothing fancy, but it was warm, and everyone seemed friendly. Colton ordered two coffees from the lady working at the counter. Minutes later, cups in hand, they found an empty table and settled in across from each other.

"Well..." Colton lifted his coffee. "Have any questions for me?" he asked before drinking.

"Lots, but I'm not sure where to start." Trisha grabbed a packet of sweetener, tore it open, and emptied it into her cup. She picked up her spoon, stirred, then took a sip. "Good coffee."

Colton smiled.

"I've been doing some research. Reading up on what to expect." She laughed. "There's a lot to learn about this business. It seems like you need to know about everything. The business end, the trainers, the jockeys, the different races. And the betting. Good grief, how do you figure all that out?"

"Takes time. It sounds like you're heading in the right direction." He took another drink. "You hungry? They make a great breakfast here. Reasonably priced and way less than you'll pay in the clubhouse."

"Maybe a smoothie or yogurt cup?"

He chuckled and stood. "They probably have yogurt, but wouldn't you like some bacon and eggs? You do eat meat?"

"Actually, bacon and eggs sound wonderful."

"Scrambled, okay?"

"Um...sure. And more coffee, please."

Colton nodded and reached for her cup, his fingers briefly touching hers. "Anything you want."

Trisha felt her cheeks heat. She blew out her breath and leaned back in her chair while watching him move toward the counter. His body proved that hard work and spending time outside created natural beauty. Colton was broad across the shoulders, slim at the hips, with long legs covered in nicely fitted jeans. "Oh, yeah, perfection," she murmured. *Whoa. Off-limits remember?* She bit her lower lip, moved her attention toward the window, gazed outside, and watched a man walk by leading a horse toward the shedrow.

After several minutes, Colton returned to the table. "Hope this is to your liking," he asked as he placed a plate of eggs, crispy bacon, and perfectly browned hash browns in front of her.

Trisha looked up and met his gaze without blinking. *You have no idea.* The words nearly escaped before she bit them back and answered, "Looks delicious. Thank you."

"You're welcome." He slid into the seat across from her and picked up his fork. "Go ahead, dig in," he told her before taking a healthy bite of his breakfast burrito.

Trisha hadn't realized how hungry she was until she took a bite and closed her eyes in appreciation. This was the best breakfast she'd eaten in...actually, she couldn't remember, but she knew it had been quite a while. Beat her usual yogurt cup.

"I'm surprised the food is so good. You know, jockeys are always watching their weight. I'd have guessed all they served here would be salad."

Colton shrugged. "Trainers and exercise people don't care about calories as much. We like to eat."

"Well, it's good." She scooped up another forkful of eggs.

"So, what do you do when not starting a horseracing business?" Colton asked between another mouthful of his burrito.

"I work for a public relations company. I promote an image. And I help my team plan fundraising events."

He nodded, seeming impressed. Then he added, "Got a boyfriend?"

She blinked. "Had one." No reason not to admit it. "Nothing serious. Besides, I'm too busy now for dating."

Colton shrugged. "Yeah, I can get that." He raised a brow. "Still, you know what they say about all work and no play."

She pushed her empty plate to the side. "Breakfast was delicious, thank you. I ate way too much."

"You're welcome." He leaned back slightly. "Changing the subject?"

She met his gaze. "I am."

"Fair enough." He held up both hands in surrender. "No personal questions."

"Thank you." She smiled.

They sat there for another half-hour as Colton gave her a crash course in horse racing. He explained the basics of a claiming race, racing conditions, and the difference between stakes and allowance races. Then he told her about the allowances for a horse's age and sex.

"My head is spinning."

"I haven't told you about lifetime conditions yet."

"Save it. I have a lot to do before the day ends, and I should have checked in at the office already. Plus, I want to start working on my business paperwork." She pushed back her chair and rose. "Thanks again for breakfast and the information."

"Anytime."

Trisha watched Colton gulp down the last of his coffee and stand. His eyes held hers for a moment before they seemed to deepen a shade bluer. Trisha shivered, and not from the chill of the front door that had just opened. *Damn. Those are some intense eyes.* She glanced toward the entrance to avoid his gaze.

Colton quickly grabbed the opened door before it closed, then stepped aside to let her pass. As she brushed by him, she caught a whiff of his aftershave. Citrus and leather, her lips curved slightly, she approved.

"See you tomorrow?"

"I'll be here," she replied.

As she walked across the parking lot, she wondered what would have happened if her father hadn't died. Would he have continued to let her believe there was no place in his life for a daughter? She took a deep breath, shoving back the emotion burning behind her eyes.

At least her father had cared enough to leave her everything he owned. Still, she couldn't help but question whether she could learn enough about horse racing to make a living, or was she being foolish like her mother had always said about him? And by the way, what was the truth about what had happened between her parents? So many questions.

She reached her car and glanced back toward the kitchen. Colton stood out front talking to a man she'd seen him acknowledge earlier. Trisha looked beyond them to the workout track, then back toward the shedrow, the main building, and farther across from the main entrance to where the street turned into this new world of horse racing. *Everything changes*, she thought. *And I'm alone in this venture. Wait. No, I'm not alone.* Colton could teach her the business. Still, she released a frustrated breath. The man was almost a stranger. Could she trust him with her future? Her brow furrowed.

She opened her car door and slid inside. She sat there momentarily and watched Colton shake the other man's hand, then take off toward the shedrow. She continued to stare at him as he walked from her sight with long, confident strides. *No mixing business with pleasure*, Trisha reminded herself. As she turned the key and backed out of her parking place, she wondered why those last thoughts about Colton kept entering her mind.

Chapter Four

"Well, damn it to Hell." Colton tossed the paper across his desk so hard he knocked the pencil holder over. Two pencils, a pen, and several paper clips scattered over the flat surface. He'd found the precise race he wanted for Icy Tears. The conditions were perfect, but Colton knew flippin' well Icy Tears couldn't win. James Ledger would enter his horse, Tribal Jack. The best they could do was run a second or, worse, hit the wire at third. That was not what he was hoping for at this time.

Releasing a loud huff, he reached for the sheet of paper and scanned through the races again. Saturday had another race that looked good, a six-furlong claimer. There was a chance Icy Tears could easily win it without breaking a sweat, but always the chance he'd get claimed.

Naturally, he thought it better to get a second or third than lose his horse, but darn it, he'd hoped to give Trisha a win on her first race. Colton scratched the back of his neck. "Oh, Hell," he muttered aloud. What was the good of owning a racehorse if you didn't run him? Besides, he could use his share of the purse money. Colton stood and headed out to secure his entry in Saturday's race. He'd have to gamble that Tribal Jack was having an off day.

Halfway to the main building, he saw Bennie Jackson, the jockey known as B.J., heading toward him.

"B.J.," Colton shouted. "Just the man I'm looking for."

"Mr. Colton," B.J. answered. A smile spread across his tanned face, and his eyebrows lifted in question as he hurried closer. "You have a horse for me?"

"I can put you on Icy Tears, fifth race tomorrow." Colton's eyes narrowed. "If you're ready and think you can get a win from him."

"I'll ride him like I stole him. No one will catch us."

Colton laughed. "That's good enough for me." Then he warned, "Be sure you make weight and absolutely no drugs."

"No, sir. Not me," B.J. quickly assured him. "No drugs. I'll make the weight. I promise," he said, placing his hand over his heart.

"Okay." Colton stared into the slender man's eyes, trying to read if he was telling the truth. "I'm taking you at your word. Come by early in the morning and breeze him. Let's have Icy Tears ready. Okay?"

"Yes, sir." B.J. nodded.

Meeting the jockey's gaze again, Colton smiled and offered B.J. his hand.

Hoping he'd made the right decision, Colton headed for the main building, where he filled out the paperwork for his entry. Now, it was in the hands of the horse Gods that everything fell into place for a safe ride and, with any luck, a decent position on the board.

With time to kill, he headed to the clubhouse, figuring he could use a decent coffee and catch up on the local gossip. It was still an hour to post time, so it wasn't busy yet like it was downstairs in general admission where the track regulars were already at the betting windows. Each person hoped their racing knowledge would pay off, and they'd leave a big winner with a pocket full of cash.

Colton walked through the door and visually swept the clubhouse. Not seeing anyone he wanted to chat with at the moment, he made his way to the bar.

"Hey, Colton. Nice to see you." The lady working at the bar offered a wide smile as she leaned across the counter. "Coffee this morning, or can I get you something stronger?"

"Coffee is just fine, Marge. Thanks."

She nodded and turned toward the barista's coffee machine. Within minutes, she returned and placed a steaming mug in front of him. "I hear you have a new owner now with Icy Tears. How's that going?"

Colton picked up the coffee and took a swig. Then, he answered her question with the only word that came to mind. "Interesting."

Marge smiled, then noticing a new person at the bar, told Colton, "Don't leave. I have something to ask you." She hurried toward the man a few seats away.

Colton nodded. He'd stick around for a few minutes. His horses had completed their morning exercise. The vet had checked the mare's leg and given his okay to start an easy workout. And he'd secured his place in tomorrow's race, so he wasn't in a hurry.

Colton leaned against the bar as he drank his coffee, letting his mind wander to Trisha and how she'd looked when he'd last seen her. Long hair fell over the curve of her shoulders while offering him a dazzling smile. Her dark eyes sparkled with interest as he talked about the racing business. And her red lips, full and ripe and oh, so kissable...she affected him like the thrill of a win, which scared him more than he wanted to admit.

"More coffee?" Marge leaned across the bar top. Her words jarred him from his thoughts.

"No, thanks," he answered, reaching for his wallet.

"Put your money away, cowboy. Coffee is on me today." Marge laughed.

Colton opened his mouth to protest, but she continued talking before he could get a word out. "You can save me a dance later. There's a party tonight at Lazy Jake's. It's

Sue's thirtieth birthday, so we're throwing her a celebration. We've got plenty of food and pitchers of beer ordered. Stop in. It'll be a blast."

"I dunno...maybe, if I'm not too tired."

"Sue will be disappointed if you don't show up. You've known her since she was a teenager."

Oh, yeah, that was true. He had known Sue for a long time. Her daddy had offered good advice if asked when he'd started as a trainer back in the day. Besides, getting out for a bit might help take his mind off the curvy woman with long dark hair and big brown eyes. He shrugged. "Yeah, okay. I'll plan to stop by." Colton smiled, thanked Marge again for the coffee, and headed toward the exit door.

"Don't forget, save me a dance."

"Yep," he replied without turning around. Hopefully, she'd forget about dancing with him. Colton figured he'd make an appearance, have a beer, say happy birthday to Sue, mingle with the racetrack crowd for a few minutes, and then sneak out. Nothing good ever happened to him at Lazy Jake's.

* * *

Trisha wanted to wear something glamorous but not seductive. After all, Lazy Jake's seemed to be primarily a casual dress

43

place. Besides, she didn't have a date, and she wasn't in the mood to attract attention to herself. Meeting a man was a complication she didn't need right now. She had enough on her plate between her new horse racing business and trying to work a full-time job. Besides, it was her friends, Scarlett and Rayna, who were the ones looking for Mr. Right tonight. Trisha stepped over a pile of rejected outfits as she returned to the closet. Finally, she decided on jeans and a soft, green-colored cashmere sweater. *This works.*

Checking herself out in the full-length mirror with her spike-heeled boots, she had to admit the look was stylish. Trisha was applying the finishing touches to her makeup when the doorbell rang. She glanced at her watch. *Shoot.* Her friends were here already. She gave one last glance in the mirror, then headed toward the front door.

"You look amazing." Scarlett gave Trisha a quick hug.

"Thanks. So do you. I love the jean skirt." Trisha smiled, comparing herself to her friend, who looked lovely. Her hair was curled and fell softly around her face. And, of course, she sparkled. Scarlett's oversized crystal hoop earrings shimmered with the movement of her head. Trisha shrugged. Maybe she should have dressed up a bit more. "I decided to go casual."

"It's Lazy Jake's. No need to dress up."

"I suppose," she muttered as she grabbed her jacket and handbag.

They had just stepped outside as Rayna pulled up out front. She killed the engine of her older model Jeep and bounded up the sidewalk. "Hey, sorry if I kept you waiting. Had to make a quick stop at the store."

"No worries," Scarlett answered. She turned to Trisha, "Let's go. I'm freezing."

"Girl, why didn't you wear a heavier coat?" Trisha fished her keys from her handbag and hit the button to unlock her car. "There's a chance of rain tonight."

"Didn't go with my outfit," Scarlett pulled the red knitted wrap tighter across the front of her low-cut blouse.

"I brought a bottle of Jack," Rayna stated as she climbed into the back seat, pulled a bottle from a paper sack, took a swig, and passed it to Scarlett.

When the bottle was offered to Trisha, she shook her head. "No thanks, I'm driving." She started her car and cranked up the heat setting.

Ten minutes later, Trisha pulled into the parking lot of Lazy Jake's and found an empty spot several rows back and on the far side of the building. She whipped between two trucks and shifted her vehicle into Park.

After one more pass of the JD bottle, they climbed out of the car and started the hike across the dirt lot toward the entrance.

Lazy Jake's was obviously the place to be on a Friday night. The bar was packed with barely enough room to navigate. Luckily, someone was just vacating a table near the dance floor, and they were quick enough to grab it. Trisha tossed her jacket over the back of her chair and adjusted the front of her sweater. "Okay. Let's get this party started. You two need a man tonight." They all burst into a fit of laughter.

Since Lazy Jake's was famous for their margaritas and were half-priced tonight, they became the drink of choice. They were on their third and feeling no pain when Trisha noticed the guy at the bar looked familiar. *Ah, crap. Colton.*

Colton McKenna stood at the bar looking even better than he had the last time she saw him at the track. Broad shoulders, a sexy smile, and wearing a Stetson instead of the usual baseball cap. *Hot damn, he cleans up nicely.*

Colton hugged a blonde sitting on a stool. As he did, Trisha's body straightened in her seat. She picked up her drink, eyes still focusing on Colton. "My horse trainer's here."

"Where?" Rayna asked as she glanced around the room.

"Over at the bar."

"Great. Let's meet this guy." Scarlett started to scoot back her chair.

"No, we don't need to talk to him. It's enough I spend every morning with him."

Rayna and Scarlett exchanged glances. Clearly, they were confused by her reaction to Colton being in the same bar as them. Well, so was Trisha. Her friends were right; she should say hi and introduce them. After all, it was no business of hers where he spent his free time.

Trisha continued to watch Colton. He stepped away from the girl he'd been hugging and glanced around. Did he sense someone ogling him? Trisha turned her gaze toward the dance floor, pretending she hadn't noticed him in case he spotted her with her friends. He probably would since they were seated smack dab next to the dance floor and straight across from the bar.

"If Colton's the hot guy wearing the cowboy hat, he's heading this way," Rayna announced.

"If he's not, I got dibs on him." Scarlett giggled.

Trisha snapped her gaze in his direction and instantly locked it directly onto him as he strolled toward their table. *Oh, damn, busted.*

Trisha didn't know if she was excited to see him or going to be sick to her stomach. *What's wrong with me?* She shifted in her chair, glanced down at her hands, and began fiddling with her napkin.

Suddenly, he loomed over her. She glanced up, meeting his intense blue eyes. As she did, a slow grin tilted the corners of his lips. He leaned closer. "I see we meet again."

Her cheeks heated, and her pulse raced. Trying to regain her composure, she stammered, "Rayna, Scarlett, this is Colton McKenna."

He nodded to each of her friends. "Evening, ladies." Then he returned his focus to Trisha—his full, unwavering attention.

"What are you doing here?" As soon as the words left her mouth, she realized how stupid she must sound. Wishing she could crawl under the table, she picked up her margarita and took a long sip through the straw.

Get it together. Get it together.

"I'm having a drink, just like you." He gave a low, husky chuckle.

She deserved that answer. Being flustered around a man was something she had never experienced. She could hold her own with any guy and had since she'd been bullied in the lunchroom back in fifth grade. Then, working the diners through high school and college, she'd backtalked the regulars and put grabby strangers in their place. Never had a man lessened her reserve unless she wanted him to. Wearing a black Stetson and a badass grin, this guy had done it with a gaze.

Trisha placed her drink back on the table. "I meant, are you here with friends?" She glanced around the room. Pretending she hadn't already seen him at the bar hugging the blonde with the long ponytail.

"It's a friend's birthday."

"I hope she's having a nice evening." Trisha blushed. "I assume it's a woman."

"It is, and I think she's having fun." Colton smiled. "Can I buy you all a drink?"

"Sure." Scarlett and Rayna both answered before Trisha could open her mouth.

"Why not," she shrugged. "If we can take you away from your date."

Colton's eyes narrowed. "No date tonight. I'm all yours, Boss Lady."

Trisha cleared her throat and then

patted the empty chair beside her. "Have a

seat."

Chapter Five

Colton wondered what was up with Trisha. She seemed uncomfortable seeing him tonight. This was confusing because he thought she'd enjoyed spending the morning with him at the track. Had he done something to offend her without realizing it? Maybe she didn't like running into him when she was out with her friends. Whatever it was, he was challenged by her disinterested vibe.

A smiling waitress appeared at their table. Colton ordered another round for the ladies and a beer for himself. As soon as the server left to give their drink orders to the bartender, Colton turned to Trisha. "I tried calling you earlier. Did you get my message?"

"Oh, no, sorry. My phone needed charging, and I guess I haven't checked for messages."

"I wanted to let you know Icy Tears is running tomorrow."

"Really!" She gripped his arm and leaned close, her sweet vanilla scent wrapping around him.

Heat slid through him as her fingers tightened, sending his pulse racing. Colton swallowed. *Damn, what was it about this woman that affected him so much?*

Scarlett screamed from across the table, "Your horse is racing! Oh, how exciting, I want to go watch."

"Me too," Rayna added. "What time?"

Colton took a steady breath. "Fifth race, why don't you all make a day of it? I'll reserve a table in the clubhouse. You'll be my guests."

Trisha removed her hand from his arm, leaned back, and gave him a wry look. "That's very generous of you. But more importantly, what are the odds of my horse winning?"

He smiled and gave the best answer he could. "There's a good chance we'll be in the winner's circle."

Trisha raised her eyebrows. "Good chance?"

"There's one horse entered who could be a problem. But your Icy Tears won't disappoint. It'll be a good race."

She seemed to relax and smiled at him.

The waitress arrived with the drinks. As soon as she left, Trisha lifted her glass. "Here's to tomorrow's race."

Colton tapped his beer bottle against her drink. "Tomorrow's race." He met her gaze. "To Icy Tears and to a safe ride."

"To Icy Tears," Scarlett and Rayna added as the four clinked glasses.

Scarlett rose. "I see someone I know. I'll be back." With a wave of her hand, she left the table. As soon as she had stepped away, a nice-looking man asked Rayna to dance, and she accepted. Within the blink of an eye, Colton and Trisha were alone.

"You look lovely tonight. Green's a good color on you." He had to curl his hands into fists to keep from touching the fabric of her sweater.

"Thanks." She smiled. "You look nice too. I like the hat."

Self-consciously, he touched the brim. "I need a haircut." His cheeks reddened. Why couldn't he just accept a compliment from her without acting like a fool?

"Whatever the reason, it's nice." She polished off the margarita, puckered her lips, and set the glass aside.

"Would you like another?"

"Oh, no. That one was already past my three-drink limit. Anymore, you might have to carry me out."

"I'd volunteer for that—"

"Hi, Colton."

He glanced up to see the pretty redhead he'd once dated standing next to him, her hand on her hip, her impressive chest angled toward him. *Oh, man. Just my luck.*

"Hi, Cara." He cleared his throat. "Trisha, have you met Cara?"

"No," she answered. "I don't believe I have."

"Trisha, this is Cara Knight. Cara, Trisha Thompson."

The back of his neck heated as he watched them shake hands, obviously sizing each other up. Cara smiled sweetly, then turned back to Colton. "I heard you have a horse running tomorrow."

"Yep. Actually, Trisha is the owner."

"Oh. Well," she offered Trisha another sugary smile. "Good luck." She directed her attention to him again. "To the both of you."

"Join us," Trisha said to Cara.

Colton inwardly groaned. This wasn't going the way he'd intended.

Cara shrugged. "Thanks, but I'm with friends." She reached over and touched his shoulder. "I just wanted to stop over and say hi." Her words were directed at him, and he knew she was offering more than a casual greeting. She was making herself available.

He forced himself to give her a polite smile. As Cara sashayed away, he took a breath to collect himself and met Trisha's curious gaze.

She stared at him for a long moment before speaking. "Girlfriend?"

He shrugged. "Not anymore. I'm unattached."

"She seemed willing to start it up again."

"Nothing to start. Hey, are you jealous?"

"Me?" She laughed. "Not a chance. We're in a strictly professional relationship. Do whatever you want."

"Okay." He leaned toward her and grinned. "Well, right now, what I want is to dance." He offered her his hand.

"You're kidding?" She frowned, her dark eyes narrowing.

"Nope." He stood and reached for her hand. "Come on. I won't bite."

After slightly hesitating, she placed her hand in his, and he led her toward the dance floor. Right on cue, the band started playing a slow tune. Colton pulled her to him, and together, they moved to the rhythm of the music.

"See, this isn't so bad," he whispered near her ear.

She gave a little nod.

He drew her closer until her head rested on his shoulder. He could smell the aroma of perfume in her hair and feel the warmth of her body close to his. As they continued to sway to the rhythm, his thoughts turned dangerous. At this moment, there was nothing professional about his feelings toward Trisha.

* * *

In his arms, desire washed over her. Their chemistry was overwhelming, and

Trisha's nerves fluttered like crazy. She cleared her throat, trying to distract her emotions. "So, what made you become a horse trainer?"

"I don't know, bred into it, I guess." He pulled her slightly closer as he executed a perfect turn.

She couldn't help but imagine how his hands would feel gliding across her skin, then his lips following that same path. She leaned back slightly and met his gaze. "I bet there's more to your story."

His shoulders lifted in a shrug. "Oh, there was a time when I was a kid, I wanted to become a horse veterinarian. But Mom had other ideas. She didn't like the ranch lifestyle. She said she wanted better for me. Those were her words: 'wanted better.' Anyway, I tried to oblige. I went to college and got a job in corporate America. Hated it."

"I can relate," Her hand glided along his shoulder, inching toward the nape of his neck. Fighting the urge to run her fingers through the hair that curled at the nape of his neck, she asked, "So, what happened?"

"Got fed up with office politics, wrote my resignation, and never looked back." He laughed softly against her cheek.

Her eyes drifted closed as she inhaled his masculine scent. She smiled while trying to imagine him sitting behind a desk that wasn't littered with racing forms.

"And here I am."

"Yes. Here you are." *Right here. Right now.* Maybe it was the tequila flowing through her body, but she wanted him like crazy.

"Am I boring you yet?"

"I doubt you'd ever bore me." She clutched him tighter. How in the world would she work closely with this man and not want to be with him sexually?

His breath was ragged in her ear as he murmured, "I'll try not to." His palm slid up and down her spine.

Her breath caught, and her nails pressed into his shoulder.

"You feel good in my arms." His words softly brushed across her cheek, and she shivered.

She looked up; their eyes met, and their gazes locked for one beat of the music.

"Hey!" Scarlett grabbed Trisha's arm, interrupting Trisha and Colton's moment.

"Come on, Rayna's riding the bull," Scarlett shouted.

"What!" Had she heard correctly?

"It's happening right now. Bring your drink." Scarlett shoved a fresh margarita into Trisha's hand.

Within seconds, the three of them were weaving their way through the crowd toward the far side of the bar. They arrived in time to witness a giggling Rayna sitting in the pit next to the mechanical bull.

The ride operator picked up his mike and shouted into it. "Thirty-five seconds! Give the little lady a round of applause."

The crowd burst into cheers as Rayna managed to stand and give an exaggerated bow to the audience.

"Up next, we have a first-time rider. Let's give a big welcome to Miss Trisha Thompson!"

Holy Hell, are you kidding me? Damn it, Rayna. Trisha waved to the ride operator. "Oh, no. I'm not about to get on that thing."

"Trisha! Trisha!" The bar crowd chanted.

Rayna ran up and pushed her forward. "Show them what you're made of girl."

Trisha glanced at Colton. His eyes were glazed as if in shock.

Scarlett raised a skeptical brow, then shaking her head, mouthed, "Don't do it."

"I'll put a stop to this." Colton moved toward the guy holding the mike. "Hey," he yelled. "She's not riding that thing."

Trisha's teeth clenched together. Memories of previous relationships surfaced. Controlling boyfriends who accused her of being too dominant, too headstrong, and too much for them to handle. Even previous bosses who'd fired her because she wouldn't go along with their creepy demands. She hadn't changed who she was for any of them, and she wasn't about to start now.

It's not Colton McKenna's place to tell me what I can or can't do.

"Hold my drink." Seething, she shoved her margarita glass into his hand, pushed past him, and into the padded pit area. She didn't look back to see his expression, but she shot Rayna with a narrow-eyed glare before jumping onto the mechanical bull.

Chapter Six

That's one crazy ass woman. The words raced across Colton's mind as he watched Trisha mount the mechanical bull. She looked like a pro, the way she bounced off the thick padded mat and swung her right leg over the metal bull's back.

Colton's breath hitched as she pushed her high-heeled boots into the stirrups, grabbed the rope with one hand, and yelled, "Ready!"

The mechanical bull started slowly, then twisted, turned, bucked, and spun. Trisha held on, the bar crowd cheered, and Colton had scenes from Urban Cowboy running through his brain. This was the craziest night he'd had in a long time...well, maybe ever.

It wasn't long before he was caught up in the frenzy. He found himself cheering along with the others as the gorgeous brunette moved in perfect rhythm to the rocking, twirling bull.

Realizing he was still holding Trisha's margarita, he looked at it momentarily, drained it in one long gulp, placed the empty glass on a nearby table, and shouted, "Ride em', cowgirl!" As an afterthought, he added, "Yee Haw!

Suddenly, things took a turn. He watched as Trisha slid from the bull and began crawling on her hands and knees to the edge of the padded pit. Jumping into action, he ran to her aid. Reaching her side, he pulled her into his arms, "Are you okay?"

"Air. I need air."

Looking into her face, he noticed her usual rosy complexion had become ashen. "Come on, let's get you outside."

Half carrying her, they headed through the crowd toward the front door. They were barely outside when she freed herself from his grip and ran toward the mock hitching post. He watched helplessly as she leaned over it and lost every margarita she had consumed.

* * *

Trisha couldn't decide if she was shaking from the music blaring through the bar's front door or if the pounding in her head had taken over her entire body.

Hands trembling, she grabbed the post rail and tried to steady herself. Sucking in a deep breath, then slowly letting it out, she closed her eyes. When she did, the earth began to spin under her feet. Opening her eyes, she turned her head and, through her blurred vision, caught Scarlett's concerned look.

"Oh, I'm sick," she moaned as her stomach churned again.

"I knew you shouldn't get on that bull." Scarlett handed her a napkin.

Trisha wiped her mouth and then whispered, "Thanks,"

Scarlett ran her hand over Trisha's arm. "Can I get you anything?"

"Something to drink."

"You want a margarita?"

Her reflexes gagged. "Lord, no! Water." She blotted her parched lips with her napkin.

"What you need is coffee," Colton stated as he stepped closer, his eyes sparkling with amusement. "I think you're drunk," his hand pushed her hair off her face.

"I never get drunk." She straightened. "I'm sick from riding that metal beast."

"Probably that, too." He laughed. "Anyway, I think it's time we get out of here. We'll come back in the morning and get your car."

"You're not taking me anywhere." She cleared her throat. She wasn't sure she could walk straight or drive her car. Still, she wasn't about to be treated like a helpless kid. "I'll get myself home."

"Ah, nope." He leaned slightly closer. "I can't let you do that."

She pursed her lips. "No?"

"No."

Scarlett interrupted, "I think you should let him. You're in no condition to drive, and neither am I. Rayna, and I can Uber home."

"Good idea." Colton agreed. "Does she have anything inside?"

"Yes." Scarlett patted Trisha's arm. "Rayna has your purse. I'll be right back. And I'll bring you water." She quickly headed back inside the bar.

Trisha's stomach rumbled, and for a second, she thought she might throw up again. When the feeling passed, she staggered away from the hitching post rail. Standing close to Colton, she raised her head to stare directly into his eyes. "I've decided to accept your kind offer of transportation." She pointed her finger. "But no funny business."

"Funny business?" He blinked. There was a momentary pause before he held up his right hand. "You've got my word."

"Good." She tilted her head and nodded as she pushed her tangled hair off her face. "That's good."

Her last memory was of him scooping her up and putting her into the passenger seat of his truck. As he buckled her seat belt, she heard him mumble something she couldn't quite understand. Then, her mind went blank.

Chapter Seven

Colton pulled into his driveway and glanced at his sleeping passenger. He drummed his fingers on the steering wheel. This was not the way he'd expected his night to go. He had few expectations of how the evening might end, but bringing a liquored-up Trisha home with him hadn't even made his list. Not that he hadn't fantasized about bringing her home, he had, just not as a reality and definitely not as passed-out from drinking.

No one had been more surprised than Colton when Trisha showed up at Lazy Jake's. His plan for the night was to have a drink with the birthday girl and go home early. Besides, Trisha still made it clear that she didn't mix business with pleasure, which, the more he thought about it, was probably a good idea. However, he couldn't deny he wished she'd change her mind.

Shaking his head regretfully, he stopped his truck, shifted into park, and shut off the engine. He turned to the sleeping woman beside him and ran his hand over his jaw. A few minutes from now, she'd be in his bed. The only problem was that he wouldn't be there with her.

He stepped out of the truck and took a deep breath. It smelled like rain—hopefully not a downpour. Icy Tears could run well enough on the wet track, but when mud clots hit his face, you never knew what he'd do. All Colton could wish for at this point was that if it did pour all night, Icy would take the lead and stay there.

Right now, he had to deal with another problem. He had to get Trisha into the house. Finally, after struggling to get her limp body unbuckled from her seat belt, he carried her inside and straight to the bedroom. She buried her face against his neck as he turned on the light and whispered, "You smell nice."

This woman is going to be the death of me.

Reaching the bed, he gently placed her down. He hadn't pulled back the covers first and wasn't about to remove any of her clothing. Glancing around, he noticed the quilt on a chair near the bed. He grabbed it and tucked it around her sleeping body.

With a step backward, he leveled a steady stare at her. She looked adorable and so damn hot. Her lips were curved in a slight smile, and her messy dark hair fanned wildly across the pillow. Resisting the urge to kiss her goodnight, he turned off the light and quietly left the bedroom.

He spent a lonely night in his guest room, tossing and turning, listening to the raindrops splatter against the windowpane before finally falling asleep. He woke before dawn, and instead of rushing out to grab a coffee and donut at the track kitchen, he filled the coffee maker with water and began scrambling eggs.

It wasn't long before he heard movement coming from the hall. He turned to see Trisha standing in the doorway, her clothes wrinkled, and her eyes noticeably swollen. On further inspection, he saw prominent dark circles underneath the puffiness, indicating the unmistakable signs of a hangover.

"Morning. Good to see you're awake."

"Don't talk so loud."

Colton fought back a smile and shrugged. "Wasn't my idea to drink tequila and ride a mechanical bull."

"Right." She rolled her eyes at him, then tilted her head, and inhaled loudly. "Is that coffee I smell?"

"Yep. Grab a cup." He pointed to the cabinet above the coffee maker."

"Thanks."

"Milk is in the fridge, and sugar is on the table."

"I'll take it black this morning." Filling a cup, she sipped and sighed. "I may live after all."

He smiled. "Have some eggs. They'll help your stomach."

She wrinkled her nose. "I'm not sure I can eat."

He scooped some onto a plate and set it on the counter. "Try a couple of bites."

She took the plate and settled on the bar stool at the kitchen island. She stared at them for a moment, then took a small bite. She chewed, swallowed, then nodded. "They're pretty good."

"Glad you approve." He watched her as she scarfed down most of the eggs before he added, "Better hurry up. We need to get your car, and I need to get to the track. We've got a busy day ahead." He drank the last swallow of his coffee and placed his empty cup in the sink.

"My car?" She groaned. "Oh, yeah. Hey, sorry I passed out on you."

"You can make it up to me tonight."

"Tonight? How so?"

"Have dinner with me." He watched her reaction. He'd purposely made it a statement, not a question. When she didn't answer, he added, "In celebration of your first horse race win."

Her eyes widened. "Today's Saturday! Icy Tears is racing this afternoon." She stood and grabbed her plate. "Oh, my gosh, I can't wait." She moved to the dishwasher, placed the dish inside, turned to him, and stated, "Don't just stand there; let's get a move on."

* * *

66

"I'm in trouble, Scarlett," Trisha said when her friend answered her phone.

"Are you in jail?" Scarlett asked, yawning.

"No. I'm on my way home from spending the night with Colton. He just dropped me off to get my car."

"Do you know what time it is?"

"Oh, sorry, yeah," She glanced toward the clock on her dashboard. "Five o'clock in the morning."

"So, who calls someone this early? Never mind. Tell me about your night."

"He was quite a gentleman. He even fixed me breakfast, and we have a dinner date tonight."

"A date. This is news from the girl who said she would never have a personal relationship with her employee. Did he kiss you?"

"No. No kissing, only polite conversation. And it's not an actual date. Just friends enjoying a celebratory dinner together. But I gotta say, he sure is sexy-looking scrambling eggs in the kitchen."

Scarlett laughed. "Nothing wrong with a guy who can cook."

"I know." Trisha smiled, remembering Colton standing in his kitchen holding the skillet of eggs. "I just hope I'm not making a mistake. I don't want to give him the wrong impression."

"I think everything will work out perfectly."

"I knew I could count on your support."

"Always."

"By the way, did you and Rayna have fun after I left last night?"

"We did. We'll tell you all about it when we see you."

"Great. Meet me at the track today?"

"Absolutely. Remind me of what time?"

"Let's meet in the clubhouse at noon." Trisha exited the parkway and turned onto the street to her house.

"We'll both be there."

"Great. And, Scarlett, I'm not screwing things up by having dinner with Colton, right?"

"I already told you you're not making a mistake. I think he's good for you. Better than the tongue ring guy from the Goth bar that you dated."

"Oh, David." Trisha laughed. "He was okay. Just no ambition."

"As I said, your horse trainer guy is more your type."

Even as Trisha listened to her friend, she still had her doubts. An image of Colton flashed into her memory. He was a gorgeous-looking man with thick dark hair, intense blue eyes, and tanned skin. Her pulse quickened just thinking about him. But was he the same as every other man she met? Seeing her as only a good time? If he was, then getting involved with him on a personal level could ruin their business relationship. Plus, if she dared admit to herself, she didn't want to get her heart broken…again. What a dilemma.

Trisha pulled into her driveway and pushed the garage door opener button as she replied to Scarlett, "See you at noon."

Chapter Eight

It was a beautiful day for a horse race. Last night's rain had cleared. Now, a sliver of sun peeked through the clouded sky, and the air was brisk but not freezing. Trisha had rushed home, grabbed a relaxing, long, hot shower, put on some clean clothes, and curled her hair. After all, her plans for today included a photo with the winning horse to hang on her wall.

Settled at Colton's reserved table in the clubhouse surrounded by her friends Scarlett and Rayna, Trisha glanced around. The area was filling up; the bar was packed, and most of the tables were full, but she didn't see Colton anywhere.

The waitress brought their drinks: Margaritas for Scarlett and Rayna and iced tea for herself. Her stomach was still a little off from all her drinking last night. She thought it best to wait until after the race. Maybe by then, she'd be ready for something more robust, perhaps with Colton, like a celebratory glass of champagne.

"So, have you seen your horse today?" Scarlett asked as she lifted her margarita glass.

"No," Trisha shrugged. "Wasn't any time since I took so long getting ready."

"That's understandable." Rayna smiled. "After last night, I'm surprised you're able to function. How's your head today?"

"Two aspirin and a long hot shower. I'm doing just fine." Trisha angled her gaze toward Rayna and scowled. "No thanks to you."

Scarlett bit her lip to keep from laughing.

"Me?" Rayna innocently batted her heavily mascaraed eyelashes. "What did I do?"

"You made me ride that flippin' mechanical bull."

"And you did us proud." Rayna laughed. "Also, got Colton to take you home with him." She pushed a lock of pink hair behind her ear. "You're welcome."

"Well...sure would have been better if I wasn't throwing up. Not to mention passing out." Trisha groaned.

"You passed out?" Rayna's eyes widened.

"Yeah. What did you do, order double shots?"

"Actually, most were triple shots." Scarlett shrugged. "Sorry."

"That certainly explains a lot." Trisha shook her head and reached for her tea. She was about to take a sip when a man approached their table. He was older, probably in his sixties, with a thick head of silver-grey hair. He was tall and dressed the part of a Southwestern businessman in his crisp white shirt, bolo string tie, and silver buckle on his tooled belt. The words silver fox flashed through her mind.

"Excuse me, you're Trisha Thompson?" The man asked, showing perfect white teeth.

Trisha nodded her head and smiled. "Yes. I'm Trisha. You are?"

"James Ledger." He extended his hand. "Nice to meet you. We have something in common today."

"We do?" Then, the name registered from her memory. Ledger owned Tribal Jack, the horse Colton was worried about beating Icy Tears. She reached out and took his hand. "Oh, yes. Our race today. I hear you have a good horse."

"As do you."

He held her hand longer than she wanted. Finally, she slipped her fingers from his grip. She knew nothing about James Ledger besides being a horse owner, but her instincts told her he wasn't a man without ulterior motives. So why was he being friendly to her?

He glanced from Trisha to Scarlett and Rayna, then back to Trisha. "May I buy you lovely ladies a drink?" Before they answered, he signaled to their waitress, motioning for her to bring another round.

"Mr. Ledger, thank you, but you really shouldn't—"

"My pleasure." He cut off Trisha's words. "We horse owners need to stick together, don't we?"

Okay, maybe he was just a friendly old guy. She'd see how nice he was after her horse beat Tribal Jack today.

Trisha offered him a polite smile as their waitress placed another round of drinks on the table.

While Scarlett and Rayna thanked him for the cocktails, she lifted her fresh iced tea and merely nodded her appreciation.

After a brief exchange of small talk, he added, "If you ever want to make some big money, consider moving your horse to my stable."

His words gave her a start. She met his gaze and answered. "Thanks. I'm happy with Colton."

James Ledger laughed and nodded. "By the way, I'm having a private party upstairs after the race. Food, drinks, music, you're welcome to stop by." He leaned closer to the table and smiled, "All of you, of course." He took a breath. "Including McKenna." He straightened. "Good luck today, Miss Trisha." He winked, turned, and walked away.

"Interesting man," Scarlett said.

"I got a bad vibe from him." Rayna grimaced.

Trisha splayed her hand. "Forget him." She lifted her glass. "Here's to Icy Tears winning today."

* * *

Nothing is prettier than a parade of frothy-mouthed, nose-snorting, Thoroughbred horses. Colton smiled as he watched Icy Tears being led around the paddock area by José. It was as if the horses knew the spectators were sizing them up. Their heads were held high, ears pointed, legs prancing. Colton smiled as he watched. *Yeah, they know they're super stars.*

Colton walked to the appointed tacking stall and waved to José to bring him in. There, they were met by two attendants. Icy Tears was a class act. While several other horses acted up, jumping and bucking, he stood quietly, letting the saddle cloth be draped across his back. Then the pad, and finally, the saddle. He stomped his leg as the girth underneath his belly was pulled tight.

"Take it easy there, big guy," Colton spoke softly while stroking the Thoroughbred's muscular neck.

José threaded the over-girth in place and then stood back, allowing one of the attendees to pull it tight. Just as it was secured, the paddock judge stepped in to check the tattoo inside Icy Tear's upper lip to ensure it matched the name on his prerace list.

Given the all-clear, Colton turned to see B.J. in navy blue and white silks walking toward them. He smiled. *Trisha should be happy. Her chosen colors arrived in time for today's race.* Giving Icy Tears a final good luck pat on his neck, he headed out to meet their jockey.

B.J. smiled. "I'm ready. I'll get us a win today."

"I'm counting on it," Colton replied. "Just keep yourself and the horse safe."

"Riders up!" The paddock judge hollered.

Colton inhaled deeply as he watched B.J. be given a leg-up, then led out onto the track. He exhaled, straightened, gave José a nod of approval, and headed toward the main grandstand area.

Where the heck is Trisha? He'd expected her to be in the paddock area with him. Maybe she'd decided to watch from upstairs along with her girlfriends. Not him. He planned to view the race from his usual spot near the finish line. Fishing his phone from his back pocket, he hit the number for Boss Lady. It rang twice before she answered.

"Where are you?"

"I'm waiting for you in the clubhouse."

"Get your behind downstairs. Unless you want to miss the thrill of your life."

"I'm on my way."

Chapter Nine

What was I thinking?

Of course, Colton would be in the paddock area, not hanging around the clubhouse. That's where she should be, as well. After all, it was her horse, and she was not about to watch Icy Tears run his first race on a televised simulcast screen. She would watch from the closest place she could get alongside Colton.

Running downstairs as fast as possible she found him leaning against the rail, eyes watching the horses as they headed toward the starting gate.

When she moved next to him, he slanted her a look. "Thought you were going to miss the live action."

"Not on your life." Trisha took a deep breath. Everything she had was riding on this race. A win could justify her decision to start a horse racing business. A loss or injury...well, she couldn't think about that. Closing her eyes, she gave a silent prayer that all went well. A safe trip around the track and, hopefully, finishing in the money. There was nothing she could do now but wait and stay hopeful.

She turned her gaze toward the direction Colton focused. Attendants were guiding each horse to the starting gate. Icy Tears had drawn the fifth position, putting him almost in the middle of the eight-horse pack.

"The last horse is loaded. Won't be long now." His voice was almost a whisper.

Trisha wasn't sure if he was talking to her or himself.

"They're off!" The announcer's voice roared over the loudspeaker.

Trisha's heart leaped to her throat as the horses left the gate.

"He broke well." Colton sounded relieved.

Trisha reached for Colton's arm and gripped so hard her fingers dug into the rough material of his jean jacket. He didn't seem to notice or try to pull away.

"He's okay. He's running third. Hold him, B.J.!" A second later, Colton screamed, "Ride him!"

Trisha let go of Colton and stepped closer to the rail, trying to get a better view. No surprise, Tribal Jack had taken the lead and ran a length in front as they circled the far side. Icy Tears still held his position of third.

They were coming down the stretch. As they did, Colton's voice boomed in her ear. "Take him to the outside now!" He shouted as if the jockey could hear him.

Trisha chewed her lips, and her heart thudded in her chest. If nothing else, she thought, horse racing is definitely exciting.

B.J. didn't have to show his mount the whip, he leaned forward, scrubbed his hand hard along the Thoroughbred's neck, and the big horse responded. Immediately, the horse and jockey moved toward the outside.

"No, why not stay on the rail? It's a shorter distance," Trisha questioned.

"Won't let him get through. It's too dangerous to try." Colton replied while never taking his eyes off the horses.

James Ledger's horse, Tribal Jack, continued to maintain the lead, but Icy Tears had moved up and was now running a close second. It was a two-horse race as they thundered past Trisha and Colton. Neck and neck, bobbing in perfect unison.

Almost there, almost there.

Trisha started jumping up and down, screaming. "Holy crap, Colton, he's going to pass him. Run. Run, Icy, run! Come on!"

The two horses crossed the finish line with Icy Tears and his jockey wearing Trisha's navy blue and white colors, a good half-length in front.

"We won," Trisha whispered as if trying to believe it happened. A beat later, she screamed, "We won!"

Scarlett and Rayna ran up beside her, waving their winning tickets. "You won!" They hollered in unison as they both grabbed her, squashing her in a hug. All three of them hopped up and down, locked together and screaming like preteen schoolgirls.

"Congratulations. Your horse ran a good race." A familiar voice cut through the screaming and laughing.

Breaking free of her two friends, she found herself staring into Colton's mesmerizing blue eyes. Still caught up in the moment, she flung her arms around his neck and kissed him with every ounce of excitement she had in her.

# # #

Five minutes had flown by like a whirlwind. Colton stood proudly in the winner's circle with an ecstatic Trisha gripping his arm. The atmosphere was electric as they waited for Icy Tears to come off the track.

He couldn't stop laughing when Trisha repeatedly whispered, "We won. We actually won."

José guided the horse and jockey within the winner's circle as the photographer swooped into his position. The big horse was still worked up from the race, but with José's strength and experienced grip, everything was under control. B.J.'s eyes gleamed excitedly as he proudly remained in the saddle ready for the winning picture.

Colton stepped over, took the leather shank from José, and then turned to Trisha.

"Want to hold him for the picture?" To Colton, his offer was more than a photo opportunity. To him, it meant a shared triumph and connection.

"I'll stand next to you."

"Okay, then, face the camera and smile."

The camera snapped with a spark of light, capturing not just an image but a snapshot of euphoria.

A grinning B.J. dismounted, leaving a trail of contagious enthusiasm as he shook hands with Colton and Trisha, then headed for the weighing scales. Next, José stripped Icy Tears of his saddle and led him to the detention barn.

"What's happening now?" Trisha asked.

Colton flashed her a smile. "Gotta make it legitimate. José's taking him to the test barn, where he'll be checked for drugs. B.J. is going to get weighed." He shrugged. "Then it's a done deal. You're officially declared the winner."

"Great. Then what happens next?"

"After that, I'm going to see that he's cooled down, has a bath, and gets his dinner, and then I'll get him bedded in for the night. You're welcome to come along or go back upstairs with your friends."

A moment passed before she answered, "I'd like to tag along with you."

"Okay then." Colton took her hand, and they walked along the path from the paddock toward the backside and shedrow. "After we care for the horses, we can have that dinner you promised me."

Trisha's dark eyes widened. "I promised? I never promised you a dinner."

"No? Somebody promised me dinner," Colton teased.

"As I recall, *you* asked me."

"Oh." Colton's eyes narrowed as if in thought. "Did you say yes?"

"I said yes."

"Good." He chuckled and gently squeezed her hand. "Then I guess I'm taking you to dinner. Come on. Let's get Icy Tears settled in for the night."

Chapter Ten

Back at the barn, Trisha watched as Colton sprayed Icy Tears with water. She released a sigh. She'd never felt sensations like the ones she felt when Colton looked at her. All it took was one glance from his intense blue eyes, and visions of him making love to her flooded her brain. And if she was being honest with herself, is that what she wanted?

Oh, she wanted it. She wanted him to move away from the horse he was bathing and walk purposely toward her. Each step would radiate confidence, a promise of the passion for coming, underscored by the deliberate unbuttoning of his shirt. The fabric would cascade down without hesitation, revealing the chiseled contours of his body.

Her imagination painted a vivid tableau of his approach, a dance of anticipation and longing. He would lift her off her feet with an effortless strength that mirrored the intensity of their connection. Setting her onto the hay bales stacked against the tack room, he'd unleash emotions that would leave her breathless.

Her hands would glide across his bare chest, feeling his muscles tense from her touch. He'd lean close and cover her mouth with his, letting his tongue part her lips. Hard and rough. Desperate to have her as much as she was desperate for him. Somehow, her clothes would disappear. She'd lean back in ecstasy as his hands ran up her thighs, then higher to reach the warm dampness between her legs.

Desire would build, taking her higher and higher. She'd find the button on his jeans and pop it open. Her hand would carefully slide into the opening of his underwear, and she'd grasp his hard erection. Her breath hitched, and she let out a sharp gasp.

"Hey, you okay over there?" Colton glanced over his shoulder as he tossed a blanket across the freshly bathed horse.

"What? Her eyes widened, and her cheeks heated like her face had burst into flames. "Uh...yeah...I'm good." She sat up straighter in the hard plastic chair she'd brought outside from the tack room earlier and lowered her head, hoping he wouldn't notice her reddened face.

"I thought you said something." He was leaning down to run his hand over the horse's front leg.

"No. Sorry. Just getting cold." She pulled her jacket tight across her chest and shivered.

"Oh, sure. Hey, you can sit in the tack room if you want. Might be warmer."

"It's okay. I'm fine." She ran her fingers through her hair while taking a deep breath, trying to regain her composure.

"We're almost done here." He stood and called, "José, take him in and give him his oats."

José came running, hooked the shank to Icy Tear's halter and took him off the walker. Colton's gaze followed the horse and groom until they were inside the stall.

Grabbing the hose again, he washed his hands then tried them with a clean towel. Smiling, he turned to Trisha, and offered her his hand. "Let's go get some chow."

She scooted from her chair and linked her finger with his. "Great idea. I'm starving."

# # #

They found a steak house near downtown Phoenix, an establishment renowned for its succulent cuts of meat and impeccable service. It was a culinary gem that had garnered a loyal following over the years. Tonight, however, its tables still needed to be occupied, allowing for an intimate dining experience that was a rarity for such a popular spot. The ambiance radiated an air of anticipation as if the restaurant was preparing for the vibrant energy that would soon fill its walls.

Having arrived before six o'clock, Colton secured a cozy booth for them near the back. This strategic timing granted them a front-row seat to watch as the restaurant gradually transformed into a bustling hub of activity. The low hum of conversations and the clinking of glasses formed a harmonious introduction to the symphony of flavors they anticipated.

Their server, dressed in a crisp white shirt and black tie, greeted them with a warm smile. Trisha wasted no time ordering a margarita on the rocks, while Colton opted for a scotch.

As soon as their drinks arrived, Colton lifted his glass and held it toward Trisha. "Here's to your first winning horse race."

"I'll drink to that," Trisha replied, her voice infused with excitement. She raised her salt-rimmed glass.

Their glasses met with a satisfying clink. With a sip of their respective drinks, they savored the evening's ambiance.

Trisha's presence managed to unravel his defenses. She possessed a blend of qualities that defied categorization. A striking beauty coupled with a quick wit, a feisty demeanor balanced by moments of vulnerability, and a mind that kept him intrigued and challenged. Colton found himself navigating uncharted territory, his heart ensnarled by the complexity of a woman who was as irresistible as the fine dining experience they were about to embark on.

His gaze lingered on Trisha, captivated by how her dark eyes sparkled in the low lighting. "You have beautiful eyes," he admitted. "They mesmerize me."

A faint blush painted her cheeks, and she momentarily shifted her gaze to her lap. A shy smile played on her lips.

I caught her off guard.

"What's the matter? Can't take a compliment?"

She leaned forward, looking straight into his eyes. "I can take anything you can dish out."

A grin tugged at the corners of his mouth. "Yeah, I bet you can."

Chapter Eleven

It was after nine by the time Trisha and Colton left the restaurant. They'd ended up spending the entire evening laughing and talking about horses. He'd surprised her by how easy he was to talk to and how knowledgeable he was about the racing industry. She'd found the subject, and him, fascinating. She was beginning to realize how much she had to learn if she wanted to become a successful racehorse owner.

Until a few months ago, Trisha had never considered owning a horse, much less a racehorse. Especially one gifted to her by a father she only knew from old family photos.

Trisha settled into the passenger seat of Colton's truck, and a sense of contentment filled the air around her. As they made an exit and headed north along Central Avenue, she sighed softly, letting the day's events play in her mind like a beautiful medley. She leaned against the worn leather seat, captivated by the vibrant cityscape lights dancing over the streets. These lights seemed brighter than usual tonight, almost like they were joining her in celebrating her first win triumph.

This night seems magical. Trisha pondered if her good mood was elevated by the margaritas she'd enjoyed with dinner or the exhilaration of her first victorious race as a horse owner. She couldn't help but smile as she considered her life's turns. When her father willed her a horse, she saw it as an opportunity for a fun, profitable business venture. Yet the emotions she'd experienced after today's victory were unexpectedly profound.

Pride swelled within her, a feeling of accomplishment that spread from her heart to her toes. Gratitude followed closely, a warm appreciation for the people who had supported her along the way—especially Colton, whose dedication and expertise as Icy Tears's trainer had guided them to this point.

"You know," she began, her voice tinged with emotion, "I can't believe how fast this has happened. I mean, from inheriting Icy Tears to today's victory...it's almost surreal."

Colton chuckled. "He's a good horse. He likes to run, and he's got a lot of wins left in him."

"Let's hope."

"He'll treat us good as long as we take care of him."

"I trust *you* to do that. Take care of him."

"That's what you pay me for."

Yes. Right, he's, my employee. She nodded. His statement was a gentle reminder that Colton was strictly off-limits for anything beyond a professional relationship. She pressed her lips together, it didn't matter, Colton wasn't her type. Though she wasn't entirely sure what her type entailed. She realized that he stood in a dark contrast to anyone she'd previously dated. Sure, he possessed rugged good looks and incredibly captivating eyes, but there were many attractive men in the world. A guy like Colton McKenna wasn't a contender for her affection. Yet, a melancholy feeling overtook her as she turned to gaze back out the passenger window.

Over the next few minutes, they rode in silence while she suppressed her thoughts of Colton and redirected her focus to her racing business. With a blend of hard work and good fortune, she envisioned turning this venture into something greater than she ever imagined. She could build her stable, wisely invest her money, and possibly take a horse to the Kentucky Derby. Her mind was a whirlwind of possibilities.

"You got quiet over there," Colton's words broke through her thoughts, pulling her back to the present.

She twisted in her seat to face him. "Oh, sorry, I'm just savoring the moment."

He grinned. "Yeah, you've had a big day."

"I know," she gushed, "It's been wonderful. Thanks for dinner, by the way. It was delicious."

"You're welcome. The first one of many more to come."

She smiled and nodded in agreement.

"Hey, are you tired?"

"Not exactly. Why?"

"I have a little ritual I like to do after a win. Care to do it with me?"

"Um, I'm intrigued." Wow. She would never have guessed him as the superstitious type. Her curiosity piqued, she asked, "What's the ritual?"

Colton chuckled, a low husky laugh that made her tingle, then answered. "It'll be a surprise."

# # #

The desert night was chilly; a crisp breeze cut through the air as Colton parked his truck in the closest area to the lake. He shut off the engine, and the quiet settled around them, punctuated only by the soft music still playing on the radio.

Colton got out, grabbed two blankets and a brown paper sack from the back seat, and then walked around to the passenger side. The cold night air caused his breath to mist before him as he extended his hand and said, "Come on, Trisha. This is what I like to do after a win. I think you'll like it."

Trisha took his hand, her fingers fitting perfectly into his grip. They walked a short distance away from his truck, soon arriving at a spot where the moonlight danced up the water's surface. He turned to face her and took a deep breath. He was about to share something he'd never shared with anyone.

Before he had second thoughts about it, he told her, "This is the place I come to after a winning race. Out here, it's peaceful, and I can reflect back on the day. Go over in my mind what I did right or wrong. Silly, I suppose."

"No. It's kinda cool. Unexpected but nice." She shivered and pulled her jacket tighter around her as she gazed out at the lake.

Colton spread one of the blankets on the ground, sat, and opened the paper sack. He retrieved a bottle of whiskey, motioned for her to sit, and then held the bottle of amber liquid toward her.

With a shrug, she settled beside him and took the offered bottle. She sipped delicately, winced, then handed it back to him. "So, when did you get the whiskey?"

"I keep it in my truck. Just for evenings like this." He draped the other blanket over her shoulders, took the bottle, and had a long drink, liking how it warmed his throat.

"Always prepared. What are you, an old boy scout?"

"I wouldn't say that." He laughed, leaned back, propped himself up with his elbow, and stared into the sky. The moon's light struggled to pierce through the thickening clouds, casting a muted glow over the landscape. After a minute, he gestured toward the lake. "Close your eyes, Trisha. Let the night and the desert speak to you. Feel the energy of today's win, your dreams, and the horses flowing through you."

They sat quietly, staring up at the sky for the next several minutes, the stillness of the night enveloping them. Until in the distance, thunder rumbled, breaking the silence.

"Looks like rain is coming. We'd better head out." Colton stood and helped Trisha to her feet. "Besides, you must be getting cold."

"Yeah, I'm ready for the heater to be on full blast." She shivered and started walking toward the truck. Colton gathered the whiskey, sack, and blankets, then hurried to catch her. Scrambling for cover, they jumped inside the truck, and he started the engine just as raindrops were beginning to patter on the windshield.

It was coming down hard when they hit the main highway. Luckily, the heater worked great on his old truck and quickly filled the interior with warm air. They spent the twenty-minute drive to Trisha's house with her constant quizzes about horses. The girl was relentless with questions.

He pulled up in front of her place and killed the engine. He resisted the urge to put his arm around her as he walked her to the front door.

"Thanks again for the wonderful day." She avoided his gaze, then looked up, her eyebrows lifted. "You want to come in? Coffee or something."

"Naw, thanks, but I'd better get going. Early day tomorrow."

"I get it."

"Stop by the track tomorrow if you have time."

"I'll see you tomorrow. Good night." She stepped inside and closed the door.

He pitifully waved at the closed door. "Night," he whispered. He turned and headed toward his truck. He couldn't believe he refused her invitation to come inside, but he knew he'd better watch his step with Trisha. She'd made it clear to him that there would be no personal relationship. Theirs would be a business arrangement only. And if he stayed any longer, he'd have to kiss her.

Chapter Twelve

When Trisha found Colton in Ardent Moment's stall, light had barely broken through the morning clouds. Her gaze settled on him as he leaned against the side wall, his attention fixed on José, who meticulously wrapped a set of protective leg wraps on the grey filly.

"Hand me the alcohol," Colton instructed without looking at her. His voice was calm and steady, with a hint of authority underlying his words.

She hesitated for a moment, taken aback by his request. "Me?"

"Yep. Right there in the bucket by your feet." His arm extended, his index finger pointing to a pail filled with an assortment of items sitting near where she stood.

She reached down, grabbed the plastic container, and held it out. "Here. One bottle of alcohol." She tried to make her voice sound playful.

Colton's fingers closed around the bottle as his eyes, a rich shade of blue in the early morning light, locked on hers and seemed to ponder something, "Want to rub her leg down?"

Trisha's heart fluttered. He had one of those husky voices that resonated from deep within, carrying a velvety timbre that wrapped around you like a cozy, warm embrace. She glanced at her recently manicured nails, then shrugged. A smile tugged at the corners of her lips. "Sure," She cleared her throat. "Why not? Can't be that hard."

José, absorbed in his task, turned his attention towards Trisha, his face breaking into a silly grin before he resumed his work.

Colton chuckled at her response and guided her toward the filly's side.

Ardent Moment's large dark eyes regarded her curiously as Trisha extended her hand carefully, allowing the horse to smell her scent. She could feel the filly's warm breath against her palm, and she offered Colton a reassuring smile before running her hand along the leg, feeling the powerful muscles beneath the skin.

"All right, get some alcohol on this cotton pad." He demonstrated, dipping a cotton pad into the bottle of alcohol. "Gently rub it on her leg, starting from the bottom and moving upward. It helps cool the muscles and prevents inflammation."

Trisha nodded, carefully imitating his actions. She dipped the cotton into the alcohol and gently rubbed the filly's leg, following Colton's instructions. The horse shifted its weight but seemed to be used to the process. As she worked, Colton stood close behind. She felt his eyes watching and glanced up to see him smiling.

"You're doing great," he said. "Take your time and keep the pressure even."

Trisha focused on the job, her nervousness gradually giving way to a growing sense of accomplishment. She was surprised by how soothing the repetitive motion of rubbing the alcohol-soaked pad onto the horse's leg was. The filly seemed to relax under her touch, lowering her head slightly.

"You've got good hands. She likes you," he said with a hint of approval.

"I've had enough massages to know what should be done." Still, she felt a sense of pride in his words. And she was actually enjoying working with the horses. Ardent Moment's leg felt solid and powerful beneath her touch, a reminder of these animals' grace and strength.

She examined the leg wraps that José had placed on the other legs. "Are these used for support?" she asked, glancing up at Colton.

He nodded; his expression thoughtful. "Yeah, they help with circulation and give some support to the tendons. It's important to keep an eye on their legs, especially after a good workout."

Trisha listened attentively as Colton explained all the various aspects of

Thoroughbred care. She was captivated by how he spoke about the animals, his passion evident in every word. As she continued to rub the filly's leg, she felt a growing connection to the horse and her new world.

"Okay, let's let José finish his job. We can go watch some workouts on the track."

Trisha stood. She looked at her hands, covered with horsehair and dirt. Colton noticed and handed her a clean rag.

"Thanks." She took the rag, wiped her hands, and tossed it into the pail. Then, pulling her phone from her back pocket, she shot off a text to her work team, letting them know she'd be unavailable most of the morning.

"I should have asked if you have somewhere to be."

"Nope, nowhere I'd rather be than watching some workouts." *Especially with you.*

"Great. Let's go." He held out his hand.

Trisha slipped her hand into his, feeling the rough callouses, the strength.

"A horse is working out this morning that I want you to see. Tribal Jack."

Right. This was a working relationship—an emotionless business arrangement. But feeling the warmth from his closeness made this hard to remember. *Focus Trisha.*

"Tribal Jack." The name registered. "Hey, we beat him."

"We did. And we'll probably race against him again. It's good to understand the competition."

"I see."

"Plus, there's another one we need to check out. I'm meeting with her owner later this morning. I may be bringing her to my stable."

"Nice. I can't wait to see her...her, right?"

As they walked, he continued, "Yep. Two-year-old first-time starter. She is full of potential, but it'll be a lot of work. Her bloodline tells us we could have a good horse."

Trisha nodded as if understanding and agreeing with everything he said. The excitement in Colton's voice was contagious, and she found herself caught up in his enthusiasm.

Colton picked up the pace, and Trisha widened her stride to keep up. The enticing aroma of fresh coffee and fried bacon floated in the air as they passed the backside kitchen. Her stomach rumbled, reminding her she hadn't eaten anything since yesterday.

"Do we have time to grab a coffee?" she asked, unable to resist the temptation of the delicious scents.

"Sure." Colton guided her toward the kitchen, a smile playing on his lips.

A few minutes later, they each had steaming cups of coffee in their hands and a bag of donuts swinging from Colton's fingers. The rich aroma of coffee mingled with the crisp morning air, and Trisha took a grateful sip. A moment of simple pleasure made her realize how much she enjoyed this unexpected adventure.

"Thanks, Dad." She whispered to herself, momentarily wishing she'd spent time with him before he'd passed. As it was, all she knew about her father was from the faded pictures she'd seen in old family albums and the descriptions given to her by others. Her mother never had any kind words. Any mention of him, and she'd find an excuse to leave the room. Trisha had finally given up asking about him.

"Horse racing might seem like all glitz and glamor, but it takes a lot of hard work and dedication." Colton's voice broke the silence between them and jarred her from her thoughts.

She tilted her head and smiled. "I'm beginning to understand. It's like you have a partnership."

"Exactly. These horses give us their all on the track. In return, we give them the best care we can."

Trisha sipped her coffee, savoring the warmth that spread through her chest. As they reached the rail, the sun was above the horizon, casting a golden hue over the scene. Trisha watched as horses and riders moved gracefully in synchronized patterns, a dance of determination and skill.

Colton handed her a donut with a playful grin. "Fuel for the soul," he said.

Trisha laughed. Taking the donut, she bit into it and chewed slowly, enjoying the sweet, sugary indulgence.

After a few minutes, she commented. "There's sure a lot more to horse racing than meets the eye."

Colton leaned against the rail with his gaze fixed on the track. "Yep. It's a world of its own. It's hard to let go once you're a part of it."

"Owners certainly seem to love their horses." Finished with her donut, she wiped her hands on the napkin and glanced around for a garbage can.

"Here." Colton held out the empty sack.

"Thanks." She stuffed the napkin into the bag and turned back to the racetrack. A big bay thundered past, his hooves throwing clumps of mud against the metal rails.

"You're right. Most owners do love their horses."

"You sound like not everyone does."

"Unfortunately, some prioritize profits over a horse's well-being."

"You mean there are people here that only care about making money?"

"It's a sad reality."

"Are they the ones who use drugs?"

He took a moment as if collecting his thoughts before continuing, "It's true. Some have used performance-enhancing drugs, trying to gain an advantage." He blew out his breath.

Trisha nodded, absorbing his words. "So, how does an owner make sure their horses are being treated well?"

He looked her straight in the face. "First of all, remember that not everyone in horse racing is bad. Most horsemen love these animals and work hard to keep them healthy. As trainers we're committed to fair competition and the best possible care."

"Good to know."

He glanced at her, his eyes appearing earnest. "If you're wondering, I'm against using substances that compromise the horse's health. It goes against the spirit of the sport."

Trisha read the dedication on his face. He was being truthful. "It's good to hear your perspective. I imagine it's not always an easy path to take."

Colton grimaced. "It's the one I've chosen. I want my legacy based on integrity and genuine care. And, by the way, it was also your daddy's way of thinking."

Trisha blinked, wondering what her father was really like. Colton seemed to have a different perspective of him than she'd been led to believe by her family.

What type of man was her father? Maybe when she felt the time was right, she'd ask Colton to tell her more about him.

They stood without speaking for a moment, staring out at the horses. "See that chestnut near the rail?" Colton pointed to a reddish-brown horse headed their way. "That's Moonlit Mirage. I'm thinking about buying her."

"She's pretty." Trisha watched the horse move closer with long, graceful strides.

Colton smiled. "Pretty won't get you far. What's important is heart."

Trisha shifted her gaze to Colton, a realization sweeping over her. In that instant, she knew that her journey into the world of horse racing was advancing before her.

* * *

Colton had to smile. Trisha turned out to be different than his first impression. Sure, she was still headstrong, but she was trying to learn the business and asked the right questions. Besides being easy on his eyes, he had begun to respect her as a businesswoman.

He glanced at his watch. It was still almost an hour before meeting with the chestnut's owner. He turned to Trisha and asked, "Want to head up to the clubhouse or stay and watch the horses?"

"Oh," she shrugged. "I like watching the horses, but I'm good either way."

"Then let's go. I've seen the horse I came to see."

"What about Tribal Jack? Did you want to watch him?"

"Another time. Come on." He reached for her hand. "I'll buy you a Bloody Mary."

Trisha raised her perfect eyebrows but didn't hesitate to take his hand. "Sounds good to me."

Colton tossed the empty donut sack and paper coffee cups in the garbage can near the walkway leading to the clubhouse. With the remnants of their impromptu snack discarded, he proceeded toward the entrance, his steps unhurried. Once there, he held the glass door open politely as Trisha entered before him. He then guided her toward the elevator, taking them to a higher level.

They entered the clubhouse and when settled at the bar, Colton signaled to the bartender. His voice carried a slight familiarity as he ordered. "We'll each have a Bloody Mary, please, Marge."

Marge, a seasoned presence behind the bar, offered a genuine smile. "Absolutely, Colton."

As their drinks were being made, Trisha asked, "So, what's the story behind the chestnut you're interested in?"

Colton curled his lips into a grin. "Well, it's a tale of determination on my part. The horse got off to a bad start. For one thing, she's scared of the starting gate. I think with the right trainer and a little patience, she'll overcome it and be a good horse. Anyway, I'd like to give her another chance."

It didn't take Marge long to return with their drinks. She placed the cocktails on the bar before them, then turned to check on her other patrons.

Trisha picked up her glass. He watched her fingers tracing the condensation along the edge for a moment before she glanced back toward him. Her gaze carried a hint of playfulness. "You feel you're the right trainer?"

"I believe I am." Colton winked, then picked up his drink and offered a silent toast.

Trisha sipped her Bloody Mary, removed the olive, popped it into her mouth, and chewed slowly, seeming deep in thought. Finally, she leaned closer and said, "I think there's something inherently inspiring about second chances, don't you?"

Interesting comment. One that could be taken several different ways. He met her gaze, wondering if they were sharing the same understanding. Was she reconsidering their relationship? He could only hope. "Absolutely. It's what we make of those chances that matter."

They stared at each other without speaking for a minute.

From the corner of his eye, he caught sight of the man he'd come here to meet. He figured he should be considerate and asked, "Are you okay alone while I speak to the horse's owner for a minute?"

Trisha's body straightened and, with a bit of ice in her voice, replied. "Are you serious? Of course, I'm fine."

He chuckled, both amused and impressed by the tone of her response. "I'll be right back. Try to stay out of trouble."

She batted her long eyelashes. "No promises."

Still smiling, Colton left her at the bar and approached the person he hoped would consider his offer for the horse. As he walked, he couldn't help but think about the twists of fate that led him to Trisha—a woman who was rapidly carving out a meaningful place in his life.

* * *

"Have you picked a winner for today?" a male voice said.

Trisha glanced up from the Bloody Mary in her hand to see James Ledger, his presence almost unnervingly close. She placed the glass down on the bar, leaned back on her stool, and offered a polite smile. "Good morning. Actually, I haven't seen the lineup for today."

His grin widened. "May I buy you a drink?" he asked, his words laced with the hint of playful invitation.

"No, thank you. I'm leaving in a minute. I have some work to finish today."

She momentarily shifted and glanced toward the table where Colton was seated.

"Well, I'm glad to run into you," he remarked enthusiastically as if their encounter was a delightful stroke of luck. "I want to invite you to a party this weekend."

"Oh, well, that's very nice of you. I'm not sure if I can make it."

His grin remained undeterred, excluding a sense of genuine interest. "Oh, you should. Give you a chance to meet some owners with big stables," he suggested, his words carrying an air of opportunity rather than intimidation. "And, of course, bring your lovely girlfriends. They'll have a good time. Even bring Colton."

"I'll ask them," she promised, becoming open to the idea.

"Good. Here's the address," he said, offering her a business card. "The party starts around five."

Trisha watched as he walked toward a couple of men standing at the end of the bar. She couldn't help but wonder about the nature of the party and the potential connections she might make. James Ledger's demeanor left her with a mix of curiosity and anticipation for the upcoming event.

It might be fun. Besides, she knew her friends would be excited. And she couldn't wait to see Colton's reaction. They'd been invited to hobnob with the rich and famous.

Chapter Thirteen

"No." Colton shoved his hands into the pockets of his jean jacket. Through the faded denim, she noticed they were curled into fists. The tension in his posture was evident, sending the message of his unyielding determination.

Trisha let out a frustrated breath, feeling her patience wear thin. "I don't understand why you won't go to Ledger's party," she pressed, her words edged with exasperation and confusion.

"The guy's a jerk," he retorted.

"So, what if he is? It doesn't mean you can't have fun with other horsemen. It could be good for business." *Why is he so stubborn? What's wrong with going to a party?*

Colton stomped into the tack room, tossed *The Daily Racing Form* on his desk, pulled out the chair, and sank into it. When he turned to face her, his normally warm blue eyes were now icy and distant. A muscle at the corner of his mouth twitched.

Trisha's irritation subsided into a weary sigh, her exasperation giving way to a sense of resignation. This morning, it had started so nicely. *What the heck happened?* She was beginning to see layers to Colton that she might never fully unravel. She stepped into the confined space of the tack room and plopped down into the chair opposite his desk.

"So, what's the plan for today?" she asked, her tone offering her willingness to move on, even if it meant sitting amid his cold behavior.

Colton's features softened. "The farrier's coming to put new shoes on Icy Tears. We've got a race for him on Saturday."

"Wow." She straightened in her chair and leaned forward, intrigued by the news. "Icy's running Saturday! Think we'll get another picture in the winner's circle?"

"That's the plan," he confirmed. "Right now, I'm waiting for a call back from the vet. The new horse is coming this afternoon, and I want her checked out."

She leaned back, her thoughts turning serious. "You didn't tell me you were getting Moonlit Mirage *today*. How did that happen so fast?"

Colton's lips curved into a genuine smile. "Yeah, surprised me too. Her owner was delivering another horse nearby today, so he's sending her as well."

"Exciting day."

He laughed.

She wasn't sure if it was at her or with her. Either way, he wouldn't spoil her excitement over her horse running another race.

"I'm going to go feed. Want to tag along?"

"Sure," she replied, her eagerness evident as she rose from her chair.

"You might get dirty," he warned playfully, his tone dancing between jest and caution.

"Don't worry about me." She laughed, stood, and firmly stated, "Give me the game plan."

It wasn't long before Colton guided her through the feeding process. Per his instructions, she scooped oats into each bucket, added a mixture of barley, flaxseed, and cracked corn, and topped it off with a large scoop of sweet feed.

When he nodded approval, she stepped back and watched him squirt vitamins into each pail, then a squeeze of vegetable oil.

"Go ahead. Use your hands and mix it up." He stepped back to give her some room.

Not one to back down from a challenge, she plunged both hands into the mixture. "Yuck."

"What did you say? I didn't quite catch it," Colton teased. His response was clearly laced with amusement.

"I said yuck," Trisha repeated. Then she flung a corn kernel at him, hitting him squarely in the chest.

"Oh, you're in trouble now, lady." Colton grabbed her and scooped her up.

Trisha shrieked in surprise while pretending to struggle to escape his grip when, in truth, she was enjoying this spontaneous exchange.

For a moment, it was just them, two friends caught in a bubble of shared amusement. But then Colton's foot caught on one of the pails, sending them catapulting across the floor. They laughed hysterically as they landed on the dirty floor, with Trisha sitting on Colton's lap, their tangled limbs and breathless chuckles connecting them most unexpectedly.

Suddenly, their eyes met, a fleeting, unguarded moment that held a promise she couldn't quite decipher. They both stopped laughing. A heartbeat passed between them. Trisha's heart seemed to join the playful rhythm of the situation, pounding in her chest. She felt a warmth creeping up her cheeks. She leaned in, almost unconsciously, her mind painting an image of what it would be like for their lips to meet.

Then reality crashed. She was his boss. "Oh," she managed to say, her voice embarrassingly shaky. Her face burned with a mixture of mortification and a strange exhilaration.

Without allowing herself to overthink it, she scrambled to her feet, brushing off the dirt from her clothes as if it could mask her sudden vulnerability. "I need to go. Bye," she blurted, her words tumbling over each other in her rush to escape the moment's intensity.

She fled from the feed room, her heart still echoing the laughter that had become more profound. Each step she took in the direction of the parking lot felt like both a retreat and an unwilling step toward an uncertain new chapter.

This can't happen. This can't happen. Trisha recited the words over and over as she ran.

* * *

It was late afternoon when the truck and trailer delivering his new horse arrived. Colton's gaze remained fixed as Moonlit Mirage emerged from the trailer. He had to admit she was a good-looking Thoroughbred. There was no denying her appeal. Her coat gleamed with a richness reminiscent of the tabasco sauce he'd generously drizzled on his breakfast burrito.

The chestnut had a broad chest and an undeniably handsome face. He couldn't help but speculate that that should make Trisha happy. She seemed to have a thing for a pretty horse. The thought of her approval made him smile. He shook his head to remove the turn his mind had taken. He needed to focus. This was business, a serious endeavor that demanded his full attention.

José stepped up, clipped a shank to the Thoroughbred's halter, and circled her around. Colton scrutinized Moonlit Mirage from every angle, assessing her potential. "Stall four," he instructed. "Make sure she has water and hay. I'll be down in a minute."

José nodded and guided the newly acquired horse toward the designated stall.

Colton shifted his attention to the driver, thanked him, shook the man's hand, and then watched him as he backed the truck out and skillfully navigated toward the exit.

He tugged his cap lower on his forehead and headed to the stall with confident strides. This filly would be a challenge, but he understood this business was riddled with uncertainties. However, this was his domain, his expertise, taught to him, in his opinion, by the best. If anyone could make Moonlit Mirage into a racehorse, it would be him.

Chapter Fourteen

Oh, for crying out loud. What the heck am I supposed to do now? This is a mess. A flippin' mess.

Trisha's head pulsed with tension. Maybe drowning her thoughts in tequila would erase the image of Colton's face from her mind. She took a big gulp of her margarita, the salt on the rim lingering on her lips.

She fixed her gaze on Scarlett and Rayna. Trisha and her friends were at the Ritz, a bar and grill near central Phoenix, their go-to spot every Thursday for happy hour. It used to be much more special when their friend, Rebecca, who worked in the law office across the street, joined them. But now that Rebecca had started her own law practice and married Mick, the guy she met in the biker bar, their get-together times were rare.

Trisha grimaced. Considering her mess, she could certainly use some of Rebecca's sound advice.

Why does Colton have to be so ridiculously good-looking? Couldn't he be some average Joe? Damnit! How on earth am I supposed to keep our relationship strictly professional if he keeps smiling at me with those tempting, kissable lips?

"Are you excited, Trisha?" Rayna's black-painted fingernail drummed a staccato beat on the table, its rhythmic sound breaking through the haze of Trisha's inner turmoil.

Trisha blinked, momentarily pulled from her reflections. "What? Sorry."

Rayna's heavily mascaraed eyes widened in a mix of exasperation and amusement. "I asked if you're excited. Hello? Your horse racing again?"

"Oh. Yeah. Well, yes," taking a deep breath, Trisha stated, "I'm definitely excited about Icy Tears." She forced aside her thoughts of Colton and got her mind back to where it should be. She had a business to manage and knew she needed to be fully present. Oh, sure, the attraction to Colton was undeniable but now wasn't the time for such distractions. She had to focus.

She needed her business to make a profit; to do this, she required top-quality horses and a skilled trainer. And at this moment, Colton was the embodiment of that expertise. She just had to remember that her relationship with Colton was strictly professional. She'd drawn a line in the sand to prevent her personal feelings from interfering with business matters. She was the employer, and Colton was the employee—a professional relationship that needed to be maintained for this venture to thrive. That would be the only way this could work.

"Think he'll win again?" Scarlett inquired as she lowered one side of her oversized sweater, unveiling a glitter-dusted shoulder.

"That's the plan. Colton seems confident." Trisha confirmed.

"Well, we'll both be there to cheer him on," Scarlett said, her optimism shining in her response, her glass raised for a toast. "To Icy Tears."

"Icy Tears." Trisha and Rayna repeated in unison.

As the conversation continued, the atmosphere lightened. Laughter and camaraderie flowed freely as they engaged in genuine enjoyment. Their waiter returned with another round of drinks. Compliments from one of the Ritz's regular patrons whose gesture hoped to make a few points with Scarlett.

The trio turned and raised their cocktails in a silent thank-you sign of appreciation to the nice-looking man sitting at the bar.

Scarlett leaned in, her voice a whisper, "Not bad. He may be my Saturday night date." She straightened with a playful smile. "Thoughts?"

"Which reminds me," Trisha interjected, breaking the conversation thread. "Saturday night. We're invited to a

BBQ. One of the hotshot horse owners invited us."

Immediately, thoughts about Scarlett's love life were forgotten.

A spark of curiosity ignited in Rayna's eyes. "That sounds interesting."

"You met him. The guy that stopped at our table the day Icy Tears beat his horse, Tribal Jack."

Rayna's memory promptly supplied the description. "That sleazy old man?"

A flicker of recognition crossed Scarlett's face. "He acted weird. I got a bad vibe."

Trisha laughed. "I know. But I hear he's the owner with the money horses."

Rayna appeared thoughtful. "Interesting. Let's go check it out. Could be your chance to network with the right people."

Trisha spoke, confidence lacing her words. "That's what I'm thinking."

Rayna inquired, "Is Colton going?"

Trisha grimaced. "No. And he told me that I shouldn't go either."

"Seriously?" Scarlett shook her head. "How did that go over with you? Colton telling you not to accept the invitation?"

"What do you think?" Trisha picked up her margarita. "You bet I'll be there. And I'm buying a new dress."

The three of them burst into laughter.

Chapter Fifteen

Horse training sucks. Colton grimaced, wiping a mixture of sweat and dust off his forehead with the back of his hand. *Why can't you become an engineer? Wear clean clothes and sit in an air-conditioned office. Not hanging around a barn with smelly animals.* His mother's words rumbled through his mind. Maybe she was right, but hey, his clothes were clean. At least, they were before Moonlit Mirage had sneezed all over him. And it hadn't helped that Icy Tears kicked his water bucket, sending water splashing all over his boots.

With a resigned sigh, he picked up the water bucket Icy Tears had sent rolling. His hand brushed against the cool metal, and he couldn't suppress a smile. Yeah, training was hard, and it was messy. It was the opposite of the sterile, artificial environments his mother spoke of. But he couldn't blame her. She'd never liked the ranch life. It just didn't seem to be her thing. She'd dreamed of a life filled with fancy parties and elegant vacations abroad.

However, when she'd met his dad, she'd been immediately attracted to the hard-working rancher who promised her a good life. But his untimely death ended her dreams. She was never the same, almost to the point of becoming a recluse. Colton couldn't help wondering how different his life might have been if circumstances had been kinder. But dwelling on what-ifs wouldn't change anything.

Colton returned to the stall and placed the freshly filled water bucket inside. The horse nickered softly, almost apologetically, as if acknowledging its earlier mischievous act. He reached out to stroke the horse's velvety nose. "You're a handful, you know that?"

Icy Tears pressed his head gently against Colton's shoulder. At that moment, he felt a deep connection not just to the horse but to the memory of his father. His dad had been a man of the outdoors, someone who found solace in the rawness of nature. He'd taught Colton to ride, to care for the animals, and to appreciate the unfiltered beauty of the world around them. It was a stark contrast to his mother's aspirations, but Colton had always felt more at home in his father's world. He was determined to honor his father's legacy to keep their shared connection alive.

Then, the fateful day when he'd met Bobby Thompson. They'd hit it off, bonding over their shared love for horses. Bobby was an experienced trainer who saw something in Colton, more than just a young man scrubbing water buckets. He recognized the fire in Colton's eyes, the determination that burned deep within.

Bobby offered Colton a job, a chance to learn the ropes and truly immerse himself in the world of Thoroughbred horse training. It was a decision that would alter the course of Colton's life. As he stepped into this new role, he realized that training these powerful animals was tough, but it was real. And Colton found the purpose he needed, and with Bobby Thompson, he'd found the mentor to teach him.

He missed his friend, Bobby. The man was more than just his employer; he'd become like an older brother, a steadfast friend, a presence Colton held in deep regard. The memories of heartfelt conversations, the wisdom exchanged, the camaraderie, and the trust. Friendships like theirs were hard to find.

A sigh escaped Colton. There were stories and some hard truths that he wanted to share with Bobby's daughter, and he knew he would someday. But the timing had to feel right...if that moment ever materialized.

With a resolute shake of his head, Colton snapped himself out of his reverie. Sentimentality had its place, but so did action. Reminiscing was for another day. Right now, he had races to prepare for, Thoroughbreds to bring into peak condition, and horse owner's dreams to fulfill.

Colton walked into the tack room and had just poured himself a cup of coffee when Bree strolled in. "You're late," he stated humorously, well aware the exercise girl was earlier than usual.

Bree rolled her eyes in mock annoyance. "Shut up." she teased. "You know I'm practically breaking records with how early I show up."

"Sure. Sure." Colton chuckled. "Don't let that fame get into your head."

"Ha. As if." A grin accompanied Bree's retort. "I want to see Moonlit Mirage. I heard she arrived yesterday."

"She's here. Stall four. And Icy Tears is running tomorrow, so make sure he gets a full workout."

She nodded, giving Colton's appearance the once over. "You've been mucking stalls?"

He sipped the hot coffee and leaned back in his chair. "Believe it or not, it's not my first time shoveling manure."

Bree burst into laughter. "Wish I'd have seen it."

Colton shook his head and grunted.

"Okay," Bree paused, her expression turning serious. "I'll make sure Icy Tears is ready for his race. What about the Queen?"

Colton nodded. "Take her out, then get Ardent Moment. Doc cleared her leg, so she's ready to get back to work."

"Got it," Bree said, her demeanor all business as she grabbed her helmet and secured it on her head. With a determined stride, she headed out, accidentally bumping into José on the way. "Come on," she told him, "Help me tack Icy up."

José glanced toward Colton, obviously looking for approval.

Colton nodded, and then, once the groom and exercise rider left, he shifted his attention back to the stack of paperwork piled on his desk. But for some reason, he couldn't concentrate. He shut his eyes briefly, attempting to regain his composure, but thoughts of Trisha flooded his brain. Her infectious smile, her laughter, and the memory of her body pressed so tantalizing close to his, almost uncomfortably close, overwhelmed him. He drew a deep, steadying breath.

Trisha was smart and headstrong, but she was also vulnerable. And James Ledger had a history of manipulating people and being involved in unscrupulous activities. There were things about the man she wasn't aware of. For instance, Ledger and Bobby Thompson had been partners until the man nearly destroyed Bobby's reputation as a trainer, and that didn't begin to cover the hard feelings left between the two. Colton carried the weight of their tangled history like a personal vendetta. And he sure wasn't about to let the man worm his way into Trisha's life.

It would be a challenge, but somehow, he needed to make her realize that James

Ledger was someone she should steer clear of, but he also knew he had to be careful. It would be a delicate balance between protecting her and still respecting her independence.

He was prepared to navigate this situation with care and caution. But to do this, he'd have to reveal the entire truth, including secrets about her father and himself. And when he did, would she trust his words?

"Good morning." A familiar voice called from the doorway.

Colton turned and looked up to see the woman who made his heart race.

* * *

"Victory Lane Stable," Trisha announced with a hint of excitement as she handed Colton the design for her new business logo, then stood back and watched his reaction. She'd spent countless hours pondering the perfect name for her horse racing business, one that would capture the essence of her dreams and aspirations. Last night, it struck like lightning. And she couldn't wait to share it with Colton. "I'm changing my Trisha Thompson LLC to this one. So, how does it sound?"

A playful grin spread across Colton's face. "Sounds like you plan on having more than one horse."

"Exactly."

He slowly shook his head. "Oh no, Trisha. Don't tell me..."

She didn't give him a chance to finish his thoughts. She interrupted, "When Icy Tears wins tomorrow, I plan to take the purse money and claim another horse."

"Is that right?" His eyes seemed to twinkle with amusement. "You realize you don't just go claim a horse without doing your homework first. We need to watch them work out on the track. Read up on their history and ask around. You don't want to end up with a lemon horse."

She scowled. He wasn't going to make fun of her goal. "Of course. I just wanted you to know my plan." She stomped to the side of his desk and leaned against the edge. "You'll start looking for one, right? A horse we can claim."

"Sure. I'll keep an eye out." He stood. "Right now, I need to focus on the ones I already have. Come on." He walked to the doorway, grabbing his cap on the way out. "Let's go watch Icy Tears workout."

Trisha stuffed the design of her new stable name into her handbag and hurried after him.

Ten minutes later, they stood shoulder to shoulder at the rail, their eyes fixed on the powerful horses as they thundered past. The morning air held a welcome contrast from the cold temperatures of just a few weeks ago. The overcast sky provided the perfect backdrop for watching the horses without the blinding glare of the early sunrise.

Turning to Colton, Trisha voiced her newfound determination. "I want to be an active owner, Colton. I want you to teach me about everything."

Colton didn't answer. He kept his attention focused on the horses.

Slightly annoyed by his seemingly uninterest in making conversation, she stated, "You know what? I'd love to be an exercise girl."

It worked. She caught his attention. He broke out laughing. "That I love to see."

"What?" She draped her arms across the rail. "I could do it."

"Yeah. You'd break a nail the first time you climbed in the saddle."

She raised her hand and glanced at her meticulously maintained long, pink-coated gel nails. *Maybe it's not such a good idea. But it's still fun to fantasize about.* She couldn't help but picture herself sitting in the saddle atop one of those gorgeous animals. "Yeah, probably right, but you'd have to admit, I'd look damn good."

"No question about that, Boss Lady. No question." He smiled a cocky little smirk that told her that he knew she was teasing.

Chapter Sixteen

Saturday Afternoon.

"Riders up!" the paddock judge yelled.

"Come on." Colton draped his arm around Trisha's shoulder and guided her from the paddock. "Let's watch near the finish line."

Trisha desperately wanted this win, needed this win. Nervously she wrung her hands and watched how the horses loaded into the starting gate. Icy Tears went in like the pro he was and stood quietly.

So far, so good.

The gate opened, and eight horses shot out.

Icy Tears broke late from his second position in the gate. Now he was pinned along the rail with several horses in front blocking his way.

"He's boxed in!" Colton shouted. "God damn it!" He slapped the racing program hard against his leg.

Trisha gasped. "What's happening?" She strained to look around the crowd of spectators, also watching intently, hoping to see their favorite get the lead. Pushing her way to the rail, her eyes scanned the field of horses. Then she caught the familiar blue and white colors of Icy Tears jockey's shirt. They were running fourth, surrounded by three other horses with no way to get through them. Blinking back tears, she grabbed Colton's arm.

Colton's jaw clenched as he continued to watch the race unfold. "Stay calm, Trisha. It's a long race. B.J.'s got a chance to make his move; he just needs to get a clear path."

Trisha held her breath as she watched the horses thunder down the track. The crowd around them erupted into cheers and shouts, but Trisha's focus was solely on her horse. They approached the final turn, and by some miracle, the horse directly in front of Icy Tears veered slightly to the right. The jockey saw his chance and leaned forward, almost laying on the horse's neck.

"Now, B.J.," Colton screamed. "Make your God damned move!"

They did. The horse and jockey surged forward with a burst of speed. The crowd's excitement grew, and Trisha's grip on Colton's arm tightened.

"Come on, boy, come on." Her voice was barely a whisper. "Get to the wire, please." She realized she was praying now rather than just cheering,

Icy Tears fought his way past one horse, then another. With every stride, he inched closer to the front horse. The finish line loomed ahead, and Trisha prayed harder than she ever had in her life. *"Run, run, please don't stop now."*

The tension in the air crackled. Trisha's heart felt like it was in her throat when, in the final moments of the race, Icy Tears caught the lead horse neck and neck. As the horses thundered past where she stood near the finish line, she screamed as loud as Colton.

He won by a nose.

"We won!" Trisha screamed.

"Hell, yeah, we did." Colton swept her up in a bear hug and swung her around in a semi-circle. Then, while grinning from ear to ear, they made a dash for the winner's circle.

* * *

Once Icy Tears was being led from the test barn, Colton headed back to the shedrow. It was a beautiful afternoon, and even better now with another win under his belt. His routine post-care was non-negotiable. Win or lose, each equine athlete under his care deserved his meticulous attention. The cooling down process started with a bath and then thirty minutes on the hot walker to help regulate their body temperature and breathing.

Pleased with how Icy Tears had come back from the race, he ran his hand along each leg feeling to see if all four were cold and tight. He nodded his approval to José and then headed to the tack room to work on more paperwork.

127

He had just finished writing José's paycheck when Trisha entered the cozy confines of the makeshift office. He didn't need to lift his gaze to recognize her presence. The alluring fragrance of her perfume signaled her arrival.

Trisha moved to the plastic folding chair beside his desk, shrugged off her jacket, and draped it over the back. Then she flopped down and crossed her long legs. "What a day. The race was so exciting."

"It was good." Colton tried to keep his eyes on her beautiful face and not on her breasts, which bounced slightly as she enthusiastically waved her hands while speaking. Colton cleared his throat and glanced back to his paperwork.

"Did my horse come back, okay?" Her concern was evident in her voice.

"Came back just fine," Colton assured her.

"Good." She leaned closer, the perfume he loved sending chills along his spine.

"So, you have dinner plans?"

"I have party plans. Remember the BBQ? I promised Rayna and Scarlett we'd go. They're both excited."

He leaned back slightly. "Are you excited to go?"

"I suppose." She shrugged. "It sounds like fun. I wish you'd come with us."

"I wish you'd forget about going."

"Colton, I don't understand the problem." The frustration in her voice was unmistakable.

"Take my word for it." He knew his reply was evasive, but it was all he wanted to share at this time.

"I can't believe you're making such a big deal about this. It's a flipping party, Colton—food, drink, conversation. Fun. You like fun, right?"

"I like fun. What I don't like is James Ledger."

"Well, that's your problem, not mine." She stood and grabbed her jacket. "You're ridiculous." She stomped out, slamming the tack room door so hard the vibration sent his cap flying from its hook.

José, witnessing the heated exchange, stepped cautiously inside the room, scratching his head. "Boss Lady's mad."

Colton handed José his pay and, with a defeated tone, mumbled. "Yep. Boss Lady's mad."

Chapter Seventeen

Trisha and her friends loved parties, and judging by the number of cars parked outside, this looked like it was a good one. With an approving nod, they made their way into the expansive room of the sprawling ranch house.

Trisha's eyes instinctively shifted to the left, where a lively gathering had formed around the custom-built bar off the kitchen area. People chatted, laughed, clinked glasses, and appeared entirely absorbed in their conversations, oblivious to the simulcast racing on the large TV screen on the far wall.

Immediately, she caught sight of their host.

A warm smile crossed James Ledger's face as he entered the room. "Well, I'm delighted to see you ladies. I wasn't entirely certain you'd make it." He graciously stepped aside and gestured for them to enter further into his home. "Please, come in."

"Thank you," Trisha replied as he took her hand and gently squeezed it.

He leaned closer. "You look lovely."

Trisha smiled, pleased he'd noticed her dress. She'd wanted to wear something nice but not fancy. The cream-colored silk slip dress, paired with red high heels and a soft red sweater, seemed perfect for a casual party.

"Congratulations on your win today. Nicely done."

She brightened instantly and couldn't contain her excitement. "That's my Icy Tears. All heart. I love him so much." Her cheeks heated slightly, and then, feeling like she might be sounding silly, gushing over her horse, she took a calming breath. "And you remember my friends, Scarlett and Rayna?"

"Of course." James Ledger replied, smoothly transitioning his attention toward Scarlett and Rayna. He took each of their hands with polite charm. "How could I forget two such captivating ladies."

With a gracious gesture, he directed the group toward the bar, where the inviting atmosphere beckoned. Smiles were exchanged as their host encouraged them to make themselves at home and enjoy the evening.

"Please, go grab a drink," he suggested. Turning their attention to the woman wearing a cowboy hat playing bartender for the evening. "Plenty of food outside, and we've got another bar set up near the pool."

"Thank you," Trisha stated, expressing her gratitude.

"Yes, thank you," Scarlett and Rayna added in unison.

As James walked away, they settled themselves at the bar and casually sipped their drinks. By the time the second round arrived, Rayna had gravitated to the pool table and engaged one of the guys from the group of men in a game.

Trisha turned to Scarlett, "Looks like it's just you and me now."

Scarlett giggled. "I could use a snack. Let's go check out the food." She slid from her seat.

Trisha simply shrugged with an agreeable smile. "Sure. Why not?"

They stepped into the backyard and looked around. Trisha had to admit that Ledger's pristine desert home provided the perfect setting for an outdoor party. String lights were strung along the eves and pathways, creating a warm starry canopy that contrasted beautifully with the dark desert sky. Cacti and native plants in terracotta pots were placed around the yard, adding to the charm.

The patio adjacent to the sparkling pool was filled with wrought-iron chairs with colorful plush cushions that looked comfortable. On the far side of the pool, a bar was set up beneath a thatched roof gazebo.

Trisha and Scarlett looked at each other wide-eyed.

"Impressive," Scarlett remarked.

"Looks like a flippin' resort." Trisha pointed to the long wooden buffet table near the outside bar.

"No kidding," Scarlett chuckled, a mischievous glint in her eyes. "Somebody's got some money."

Trisha nodded. "I guess Ledger does have some good horses."

"Come on. I'm starving." Scarlett took Trisha's arm and pulled her toward the irresistible savory smell of barbecue.

Trisha's eyes scanned the feast laid out before them. The table was elegantly lit with candles and lanterns. Her mouth began to water as she took in all the trays of barbecued meats, the numerous side dishes, colorful salads, and the beautiful display of desserts.

She picked up a plate and began to fill it with samples of almost everything. Then, finding a vacant table, they settled down to enjoy their food. As they ate, they observed the rest of the setting. The open desert terrain was peppered with seating areas featuring rustic wooden benches and Adirondack chairs around firepits. Someone was strumming on a guitar on the other side of the pool as folks gathered around.

"Quite a shindig," Scarlett voiced as she wiped her hands on a napkin.

Trisha nodded in agreement. "I'm truly impressed. The guy may be a bit sleazy, but he isn't pretending to have money."

Picking up her drink, Trisha turned her attention to the pool, watching how the overhead lights danced across the water. She released a long sigh.

"Are you okay," Scarlett asked. "You seem distant."

"No. I'm fine. I was thinking about why Colton wouldn't come tonight. I mean, seriously, why is he so stubborn about James Ledger?"

Scarlett furrowed her brows. "Have you asked him?"

Trisha sighed. "Sorta. He never gives me a straight answer. He just gets mad and starts yelling."

Scarlett nodded as if understanding the complexity of the problem. "Interesting. Must be something in their history." She stood up, collected their empty plates, and tossed them into a nearby container. "I'm going to get us another drink."

Left alone momentarily, Trisha leaned back in her chair, her thoughts drifting as she gazed up into the star-studded sky. Memories of the night she spent with Colton at the lake flooded her mind. She closed her eyes and smiled. Suddenly feeling the presence of someone standing next to the table, she opened her eyes and glanced up.

"You look deep in thought," James Ledger said with a smile.

She laughed nervously as she straightened in her chair. "I was just reliving today's race." That was only a tiny lie.

James slid into the empty chair next to Trisha. "I hope you're enjoying yourself."

"Oh, yes. Your party's lovely. The food was delicious. And I ate way too much."

He nodded. "I'm glad."

She reached for her drink and took a sip.

"How's your drink? May I get you a refill?"

"No, thank you. Scarlett's getting me another."

He nodded. "So, how's business? Are you thinking about adding more horses to your stable?"

"I'd love to expand, and maybe someday I will. I'm finding out racehorses are an expensive encounter." She laughed. "Of course, you already know that."

"If you ever need any advice, I'm here for you."

"I'll keep that in mind."

"And if you ever want to sell Icy Tears, I'll give you a good price for him."

"I love Icy Tears. I'll never sell him."

James leaned in closer, his tone thoughtful. "No? What about when his racing career is over? He doesn't have the breeding to be a stud."

"I guess, I don't know," she admitted.

"Something to think about. He's not a puppy, Trisha. You need to treat him like what he is, he's an investment. Make the cash while you can. With the right trainer, you could make yourself some *real* money."

Trisha raised her eyebrows, sensing his intentions. "You're referring to yours?"

A confident smile crossed his face. "I'm known to employ the best of the best."

"I have a good trainer," Trisha blurted, feeling the need to defend Colton.

James chuckled as he lifted a hand in a defeated signal. "Don't get me wrong, Trisha. I'm not saying he's incompetent at all. Colton is a very knowledgeable horse trainer, but he lacks the drive. He only sees himself as small time."

Trisha stiffened. "I think you're wrong. I don't see Colton as small time at all."

"Oh, you will." His face seemed to be tense. "My stable is always open to you. Please come visit. Let me show you what a successful horse operation looks like."

Trisha found herself grappling for an answer. She clenched her fist under the table to control the urge to punch him.

At that moment, Scarlett arrived with fresh drinks. She sat them on the table and glanced between the two with a confused expression.

James stood. "You'll excuse me. I have some guests to check on." He smiled at Scarlett, patted her arm, and then turned to Trisha. "Think about it, Trisha. I can make you a rich woman."

As James walked away, Scarlett slid into the chair and asked, "What was that all about?" Her concern was evident.

"I'm not sure." Trisha picked up her fresh drink and slowly sipped.

Scarlett pressed, "Did I hear him right? He wants to make you rich?"

"Yeah. But I got a weird feeling there's a big price to pay in return," she admitted as a shiver of uncertainty ran along her spine.

Scarlett let out a soft gasp as she glanced over to where James stood laughing with some guests. Scarlett turned back to Trisha, a distressed look showing in her eyes. "Should I be worried about you?"

"Nope. Nothing I can't handle."

Scarlet frowned. "I hope so."

Trisha leaned back and sipped her drink. Her eyes focused on Ledger as he stood chatting with friends. He seemed nice enough. But she couldn't help but wonder what was really behind all the kindness he was showing. She couldn't shake the uneasy feeling he gave her.

A second later, a nice-looking man with a neatly trimmed beard and striking blue eyes approached their table.

Scarlett introduced him as Paul, a guy she'd met while getting their drinks.

Trisha offered Scarlett's new friend a bright smile.

Paul reached for Scarlett's hand. "You promised me a dance."

"I'd love to." She rose, casting a quick glance toward Trisha. "Mind if I leave you alone for a bit?"

Trisha nodded. "No problem. Go have fun."

Scarlett's words had been more of a statement than a request. She leaned back and smiled as she watched the happy couple stroll away hand in hand. Rayna was still in the house with the pool table guy. It seemed like her friends were having a great time. She released a deep sigh and then sipped her cocktail. *At least the drinks are good.*

The night air had turned cooler, sending a shiver down Trisha's spine. She wrapped her sweater tighter around her shoulders and gazed into the distance. The party was getting rowdier by the minute. Laughter and animated conversations filled the air while a group of energic souls, Scarlett included, danced with reckless abandon in the makeshift dance area near the outdoor bar. As she took another sip of the margarita, she couldn't help but feel a pang of isolation. Surrounded by a crowd of people, an unexpected wave of loneliness washed over her.

She swirled her drink as her thoughts drifted to Colton. Staring into the star-sprinkled sky, his image materialized in her mind. His intense blue eyes and his dark hair that always seemed mussed and flattened to his head when he removed his baseball cap. Memories of their conversations, their laughter, and the moments of quiet time together began to resurface.

Could two people who worked together also have a personal connection? It wasn't an entirely new concept. "Lots of people work together and have a great relationship, right?" she mused aloud as if trying to justify her growing feelings. She thought about the countless married couples she knew who successfully owned businesses together, their lives seamlessly blending work and love.

Seriously, just because I had a bad workplace experience years ago doesn't mean history has to repeat itself. Would it hurt me to have a little fun?

She and Colton were both adults, mature enough to handle whatever might happen. If things didn't work out, well, they'd deal with it like responsible grown-ups.

So, what am I doing sitting here?

She informed Scarlett and Rayna of her plan, then downed the remainder of her margarita. As the tangy taste of lime and tequila slid down her throat, she felt a spark of excitement. Despite the fact James Ledger's party was still going full swing, she slipped out and called an Uber.

Chapter Eighteen

It was after ten p.m. No wonder Colton was tired. His day had started at five this morning, and José needed to leave early this afternoon, so all the evening chores had landed in his lap. Not that he had anything better to do, in fact, it was a welcome distraction. It kept the relentless, intrusive thoughts at bay. Thoughts that tended to wander into forbidden territory. Namely, the captivating brunette with the big brown eyes. *Damn it. Why did she have to be so headstrong?*

He made a quick pit stop at a local drive-thru and ordered a double meat burger complete with oozing cheese and crispy bacon. He also added a large size order of golden-brown fries. Just thinking about the salty potatoes made his mouth water. Thankfully, he'd be eating soon, he thought as he turned onto the street where his home was located.

He pulled into the driveway and hit the remote button. The garage door lifted. A few seconds later, he walked into his kitchen, tossed the brown bag on the counter, headed straight to the refrigerator, and grabbed an ice-cold beer.

Fifteen minutes and a quick shower later, Colton was settled on the couch in front of the flat-screen TV mounted above a gas fireplace, a burger in one hand and a long-necked beer in the other. Luckily, an action-filled movie he'd hoped to catch had just started. As he sank his teeth into the burger, Colton felt the stresses of the day melting away, at least for the moment, leaving him with nothing but the film's excitement and the tantalizing aroma of his meal.

Finished with his food, he leaned back on the comfortable couch ready to enjoy the ending of the movie. After several minutes his eyelids closed.

Startled by the sound of the doorbell, he groggily rubbed his eyes and glanced at his watch. He must have dozed off. The room was quiet except for the TV now showing an old sitcom rerun and the doorbell ringing for the second time.

"Yeah, yeah, I'm coming." He slowly headed to the door. *Somebody better have a good reason to bother me in the middle of the night.*

He checked the peephole and did a double-take before opening it.

"Hi." Trisha stood under the light from his porch. She shrugged. "I tried to call."

"Oh, I,.uh,.I guess I left my phone in the truck." He blinked, self-conscious of how he was dressed. After his shower, he'd thrown on a pair of baggy sweatpants and an old, faded T-shirt. Plus, he was barefoot.

"Oh, well, that's probably why you didn't answer."

"Yeah. Hey, are you okay?" He ran his hand through his hair.

A smile spread across her face. "I'm fine. May I come in?"

"Yes. Sorry. .uh. .of course. Please come in." He stepped back and opened the door wider. As she passed, he caught the scent of her perfume. He loved how she wore just enough to entice him, not overpowering like some he'd known. Damn, she took his breath away every time he looked at her.

"Have a seat," he motioned toward the couch. Then he quickly scooped up the clutter of fast-food containers and the empty beer bottle from the coffee table. "Sorry about the mess."

"Not a problem."

"Can I get you anything?" He called from the kitchen as he dumped his garbage into the trash.

"I'm good. Thanks."

"All right," he said as he walked back and slid onto the couch beside her. "So, what do I owe this visit? Have you come up with another idea you couldn't wait to lay on me?"

"Nope. Just wanted to see you."

Her words surprised him. Why did she want to see him at this hour? Was there something she wasn't telling him? He struggled to respond. "I thought you'd be having fun at the party tonight."

"Yeah, I went." She shrugged. "I left."

"I'm glad." He blurted before he had time to think about how it might sound.

"Are you?"

"Yes," he replied slowly. That was the truth. He saw no point in hiding his feelings. He'd made them clear to her already.

"Glad I left the party or glad to see me?" She removed her sweater, revealing her bare shoulders and the low-cut neckline of her dress. She leaned slightly toward him.

Colton immediately noticed how her dress molded against her breasts, outlining her pert nipples. Mesmerized, he cleared his throat. Her presence unnerved him. "Both." He couldn't stop staring at her. She looked so beautiful.

Forcing his eyes upward, his gaze locked on her crimson lips, imagining how soft they'd feel against his own. He'd never believed in love at first sight, but ever since the first day he'd met her, he'd found it hard to stop thinking about her.

Leaning even closer, she whispered, "I think you missed me."

Her whisper made his body pulsate. "That's what you think?" He placed his hand lightly on her thigh. She put her hand on top of his and scooted closer until her hip pressed against his. Her short, silky dress crept higher and higher up her thighs as she snuggled beside him.

"Damn, you look pretty. I've been thinking about you all night." Not a lie.

"I've been thinking about you too. That's why I'm here."

"So, you really did come over because you wanted to see me?"

"I already told you that, Colton." She draped one leg across his lap.

Colton raised his eyebrows, shocked by her aggressiveness. What had gotten into her? Not that he minded. Nope, he didn't mind it one bit. He just wasn't sure what was happening. Without thinking, he gently ran his hand slowly along her bare leg. "I like the red shoes."

"They're starting to hurt. Take them off for me." She wiggled her foot.

He didn't hesitate. He unbuckled the strap around her ankle and slowly removed her shoe. As it fell to the floor, she placed her other leg across his thighs indicating she wanted that one removed as well. Obliging, he removed the other high heel and gently rubbed the top of her manicured feet.

His mind was still reeling, trying to figure out what was happening. Trisha was acting entirely out of character. But man, oh man, he liked the direction her mind was taking.

Before he could pull his thoughts together, she moved her legs from his, placed her hands on his chest, and pushed him back against the couch. Colton's breath caught in his throat as she climbed into his lap, straddling him, and pressed her lips to his.

He braced his hands on both her hips as her fingers dug into his shoulders, and her body seductively rocked on the bulge she'd created in his pants.

Suddenly, she pulled away and stared into his eyes. "I shouldn't want you."

"But you do," he replied as his erection increased, pushing against the material of his sweatpants.

"Oh. Yes, I do," she whispered. Her breath was warm against his cheek.

"So, what are we going to do about it?"

"I'm ready for a suggestion."

"I have an idea." He ran his finger along her cheek, cupped her chin, and tilted her face slightly. He leaned in and pressed his mouth to hers. *She's going to stop this any minute. Don't get carried away.* But as his lips touched hers, all rational thoughts in his lust-fogged brain were gone. Breaking their kiss enough to speak, he told her, "I want you, Baby. If you want me to stop, tell me now."

"Don't stop. Please, Colton."

Kissing her deeply again his hands slowly moved higher along her thighs. As per her invitation, he slid his fingers along the edge of her panties. She moaned against his mouth and started showering him with hot kisses over his cheek and down his neck all the while making circling motions with her hips.

He continued to touch the lacey seam of her panties, feeling the dampness between her legs. She straightened and pushed the narrow straps of her dress off her shoulders. The soft material slid down, setting her ample breasts free. Trisha arched back, giving him a perfect view, then cupped each one in her hands, pushed them together, and pressed them to his mouth.

I've died and gone to heaven.

Hungrily he sucked the pink nipples that peaked to perfection as he nipped and licked the first one, then the other trying to fit them both in his mouth. As he did, his finger quickly slipped underneath the lacy fabric to touch her hot, wet flesh.

He was so hard now he ached. His finger eased into her, and when he did, she touched her forehead to his and rocked against his hand.

He wasn't sure how much more he could take. Tonight was blowing his mind. He'd been with many women, but none made him feel like this woman did.

Her scent enveloped him as his fingers increased the pace, his thumb touching her with steady pressure. He tilted back and shut his eyes when suddenly she leaned forward and crushed her mouth against his as she pulsated around his fingers.

Trisha lifted herself off Colton and stood beside the couch, letting her rumpled dress fall to the floor. She was left wearing only her lace undies. His hand reached out, slipped his finger under the lace, and pulled her closer. Her body tingled as his strong hands moved along her hips.

"Let's get rid of these," he said as he slowly rolled her panties down her legs. She stepped out of them and kicked them aside. Now, she was completely naked. She sucked in a breath as she watched his eyes roam over her body.

"God, you're beautiful." He leaned forward, skimmed his warm lips over her tingling skin, and moved downward.

A low moan escaped her throat. He grabbed both her arms and pulled her onto the couch beside him, then leaning over her, he kissed her, his tongue delving deep, exploring her mouth. Her insides sizzled again.

Her hand slid between them, loosened the string of his sweats, and slowly pushed them down. Finding the opening of his underwear, she grabbed the thick shaft and, lifting her hips, began rubbing the tip on her opening.

Pulling away from his mouth enough to speak, she whispered, "Colton, I need you inside me. Take me now." Her body felt like she might ignite if he didn't. Never had she wanted anyone like this. "Please," she begged as she squirmed beneath him.

"Baby," he whispered, his voice sounding heavy with arousal as he pushed into her.

Trisha gasped. His hands grabbed her legs and wrapped them around his waist, angling her hips upward, shoving deeper inside her. She squeezed her eyes closed, completely lost in the sensations of him filling her so completely.

They moved together at a feverish pace. It was as if she couldn't get enough of him. Her fingers curled into the couch material as she lifted her hips, trying to press tighter against him. She'd never felt like this. So lost in the emotions of just feeling, not thinking of anything but his body plunging into hers. "Now, Colton. Harder."

He obliged her, increasing his movements. He lifted her hips and pushed deeper and faster. Above her, she heard his growl, "Oh, God, Trisha."

When Colton collapsed on her, she wrapped her arms around him, clinging tight as her body returned to normal. "Wow, you could become addictive." Trisha panted, trying to get control of her breathing.

They lay locked in each other's arms for several minutes before Colton eased himself from her, then stood staring at her with an unreadable look on his face.

Aware of her nakedness, she felt herself blush. "Colton, this isn't something—"

"I know." He cut off her words.

What does he know? Did he understand this wasn't how she usually acted? She pulled herself into a sitting position. "It's late. I should go."

He reached over and brushed a damp curl from her forehead. "Oh, Lady, we're just getting started."

Before she could answer, he scooped her up and carried her toward his bedroom.

Chapter Nineteen

Trisha woke to the decadent aroma of coffee. As her senses slowly aroused from a deep sleep, she rolled onto her side, her heart quickening as she realized she was alone in an unfamiliar bed. The room was cloaked in a soft, dim light seeping through the closed shutters covering the bedroom window. Then it all came rushing back to her—*Colton*. Her mind swirled with emotions. Last night, she and he had changed from a friendly employer and employee to lovers.

A wave of delightful shivers coursed through her as she remembered their lovemaking. The memory of all the places his lips had touched her. Wow, the man knew how to make love to a woman. He was amazing. And intelligent and good-looking and an excellent horse trainer. He was perfect.

The statement made her smile fade. But could their relationship work? Did they even have a personal relationship? Was this a sexual opportunity for him? A hot flush of unease flowed through her body as she remembered how she'd impulsively shown up at his place and practically thrown herself at him when he opened the door. She sighed heavily. Had she ruined everything between them?

But then her mind wandered to the memory of his touch. The way he'd held her. The words he'd whispered at precisely the right moments. It had to have meant more to him than just a one-night fling. She frowned. *It just had to have.*

A sudden noise from the adjacent room startled her. She sat up in bed and turned toward the door just as Colton stepped into the bedroom, a steaming mug in his hand.

"Hey, you're awake?" His voice carried a hint of tenderness. "I tried to be quiet and let you sleep." He placed the mug on the oak nightstand next to the bed. "Thought you might like some coffee."

A smile stretched her mouth as she propped her back against a plush pillow and pulled the comforter over her naked body. "I'd love coffee. Thank you."

"You're welcome." He eased onto the bed near her knees. "How do you feel this morning?"

Her cheeks heated from the emotions swirling beneath the surface. She looked into his eyes. "I feel slightly embarrassed." She glanced down and pressed her lips together.

"Embarrassed?" His voice was soft, almost soothing, as he reached for her hand.

"No, Trisha, you have nothing to be embarrassed about."

"I don't want you to think I always act like I did last night," she admitted. "You know, showing up in the middle of the night, expecting a guy to...to...you know, do what we did."

"Look at me, Trisha." He scooted closer, his touch gentle as he cupped her chin in his strong hand. "I know you. Better than you think. Nothing made me happier than what happened last night. You can trust me. It was wonderful."

"Yeah?" Her voice wavered slightly.

"Yeah." His smile mirrored the sincerity in his words. "I don't want this to be a one-night stand."

"Neither do I." She brushed a tear away that attempted to slide down her cheek.

"Good." He leaned in, placing a kiss on her lips before pulling back and standing up. "So, drink your coffee." He pointed toward the nightstand and then turned for the doorway. "I gotta go to work."

"Can you drop me at my house?" She smiled when he nodded that he would. She pushed her hair back off her face and then reached for the mug, but as she took a sip of the warm brew, she remembered she only had a wrinkled cocktail dress and stilettos to put on. *Crap. At least I have a sweater.*

* * *

Satisfied that all the horses had been groomed and fed and each stall had been cleaned, Colton headed to his tack room/makeshift office. The idea of brewing a cup of coffee briefly crossed his mind, but he promptly dismissed it. Three cups already had made his nerves jittery enough. He didn't need more caffeine. He decided he'd wait until lunchtime before he had another.

He settled into his worn desk chair and let his tired eyes scan the stack of paperwork before him. As he did, frustration welled up inside him, and he couldn't help but let out an audible groan. The last thing he wanted to do right now was deal with this pile of administrative work. His thoughts kept drifting to Trisha.

He leaned back and closed his eyes, picturing the gorgeous brunette with the big brown eyes, and allowed the memories of last night to wash over him like a warm embrace.

When he opened the door last night, he'd thought he was dreaming. Trisha stood before him, looking radiant under the light from the porch, her eyes sparkling even more than usual. Then, later, touching her creamy skin, her body molded to him. She was indeed the perfection he'd never known. Trisha awakened feelings in him that he struggled to define. Love? It must be love that he felt. He couldn't stop thinking about her and knew he'd do whatever it took to keep her in his life.

Colton blinked as he returned to the present. Their new personal relationship presented a problem. He reached up and raked his hand through his hair, an outward reflection of his inner turmoil. He'd made a solemn promise to Trisha's father, one he intended to uphold. Yet, to keep that promise, he realized he'd have to keep certain truths from her about himself. Their relationship had changed dramatically last night, deepening the complexities of his situation. Now, he was trapped between conflicting choices with no easy way out.

Colton exhaled slowly, feeling the weight of his decisions pressing down on him. On the one hand, honesty might cause Trisha to view him differently and potentially shatter the new bond they were forming. Plus, she could believe every unscrupulous thing her family had told her about her father. On the other hand, keeping secrets from her ran against his principles. Colton found himself torn, grappling with the agonizing decision. Keep his promise to a dying man or keep secrets from the woman he was falling deeply in love with, knowing that either of the paths he chose would leave him with a heavy heart.

Chapter Twenty

The first thing Trisha did after Colton dropped her at her house was take a long, hot shower. Her choice of lavender-scented body soap and vanilla shampoo worked their magic to refresh and revitalize her senses. Wrapped in a fluffy white robe, she padded barefoot into her bedroom and sank onto her bed. With her head nestled in the pillow, she closed her eyes and pictured Colton in her mind. A wistful sigh escaped her as she mused, could last night have been any better?

Trisha opened her eyes and blinked. Sunlight streamed through the blinds, bringing her back to the present. Yawning, she reached for her phone, which sat charging on the nightstand, and checked the time. It displayed 11:40.

Good heavens, it's almost noon. Surprised by the realization that she had dozed off, Trisha sat up in bed, stretched, and immediately called her friend.

"Scarlett, you'll never guess what happened last night."

"You went to Colton's?"

"Yes! It was fantastic. God, he's amazing." Trisha giggled. She removed the towel from her hair and ran her hand through the damp tangles as she continued, "he drove me home on his way to the track this morning. Remember I'd taken an Uber from the party."

"I do remember, and I can't wait to hear everything. I bet he was surprised when you showed up at his doorstep."

Trisha let out a big sigh. "Yeah, but now, I'm confused. I mean, after sex how am I supposed to act around him? I'm still his employer, but I really am crazy about him. I want a personal relationship. What if he doesn't feel the same about me? What do I do then?"

"Look, the guy's wild about you. It's written all over his face. Act like you always do, and everything will be fine. Talk to him about your concerns. You can work it out."

"You think."

"I definitely think so." She smiled. "Oh, and, by the way, Rebecca invited us to Mo's tonight. She's planning on going and wants us to meet her."

"Sure. Hey, I'll bring Colton."

"Great. See you tonight."

With Scarlett's reassuring words in mind, Trisha disconnected the call. Her thoughts now focused on navigating the uncharted waters of her newfound connection with Colton.

Two hours past his usual bedtime, Colton found himself, along with Trisha, entering an unfamiliar and raucous setting of a crowded biker bar. The air was thick with the pungent mix of cigarette smoke and the unmistakable aroma of beer. Neon lights flashed and pulsed, casting surreal shadows in the dimly lit establishment. The relentless sound of blaring music pounded in his ears, making him wonder how in the world he ended up here. Then he glanced at Trisha in her tight jeans and immediately remembered. He was a sucker for a woman with beautiful curves, especially this one.

On the right side of the bar, a live band stationed on a makeshift stage was winding down from their current country tune. The lead guitarist plucked the final notes of a soulful solo, and the drummer executed a dramatic flourish before they took a bow. The crowd erupted in cheers and applause, filling the space with a chaotic symphony of excitement.

Trisha navigated them through the sea of leather-clad patrons toward a corner booth. As they approached, he noticed two individuals already seated. The woman he immediately recognized as Trisha's red-haired friend, Scarlett.

A burly man was seated beside Scarlett, his face half concealed by a long beard flowing down his broad chest. He wore a weathered denim jacket adorned with an assortment of biker patches, each one, no doubt, telling a story. Despite the intimidating exterior, his eyes bore a warmth that contrasted with his rugged appearance.

The moment Scarlett spotted them, she waved enthusiastically. As Colton settled into the booth, he couldn't help but feel a mix of excitement and trepidation. This unexpected date with Trisha and her friends in a rowdy biker bar promised to be an unforgettable night.

Introductions were made, and he discovered that Henry was also a bouncer here at Mo's. Henry's shift had ended early tonight, and he'd happily agreed to hang out with Scarlett and her friends. Scarlett told him how Rayna was behind the bar this evening because Mick, the owner and husband to their friend Rebecca, ended up short-handed tonight. Oh, and she'd quickly added Mick was also the guitarist and lead singer in the band.

Trisha squeezed his hand. "You'll have it all straight before the night's over."

"Right." He nodded and leaned closer, inhaling her sweet, familiar scent.

A waitress appeared, and they ordered wings, burgers, and two pitchers of beer for the table. While waiting for the food and drinks, they made small talk.

"I hear you train horses for the racetrack, Colton. How's that going?" Henry asked, his voice sounding sincere.

"Good as can be expected, I guess. Just trying to make a living."

Henry nodded. "Aren't we all?" He angled his head. "So, how long can you expect a horse to run before he has to retire? I've always wondered about that."

"Depends." Colton paused for a minute, trying to answer as best he could. "The trainer has a lot to do with it. Good trainers can keep a horse sound longer than others."

"Sound?" Scarlett questioned.

"Sound means fit, not sore or broken down. A horse is an athlete and must be in shape to run a good race." Colton smiled.

"I never thought of horses as athletes. But I guess they really are," Scarlett stated.

Colton continued to explain, enjoying the opportunity to share his passion for horse racing. "Absolutely, Scarlett. Horses need the right diet, exercise, and care. It's like any professional sport, except they can't tell us when something is wrong."

Trisha chimed in, and Colton noticed the glint of pride in her eyes. "Colton's good at understanding what a horse needs."

Henry nodded thoughtfully. "Seems like a challenging but rewarding job."

"Oh, it is, but you know what's most important?" Colton smiled, then paused for a dramatic effect. "Luck."

They all laughed along with him as their food and drinks arrived. Trisha asked for an extra mug, explaining they had another friend joining them. Scarlett poured the pitchers of beer into frosty mugs and passed them around. All four raised their drinks for a toast.

"To an evening filled with laughter and adventure," Trisha proposed.

"And to friends," Scarlett added.

"To friends," Colton, Henry, Trisha, and Scarlett spoke in unison, clinking their glasses together in a heartfelt toast.

As the conversation flowed, Colton learned more about Trisha's friends. Scarlett's recent hobby was photography. She worked for a real estate developer and loved it when they let her take photographs of new projects. Henry had a background in construction, working on heavy equipment, and had been a bouncer at Mo's for some time.

Colton was about to sip his beer when Trisha's face lit up, and she screamed, "Rebecca." She slid out of the booth and wrapped her arms around a slim blonde woman in a hug.

"Must be Rebecca," Colton observed, turning to Henry.

Henry smiled and nodded as Scarlett rose from her seat and joined the hugs.

Rebecca was exactly as Trisha had described her. Lovely, slender, and possessing a solid presence that belied her delicate appearance. She excluded confidence and didn't appear to be someone to be underestimated, dressed in a formfitting white skirt and matching sweater.

"Colton, this is Rebecca," Trisha introduced her friend.

"Hello, Rebecca." He held out his hand.

"Nice to meet you," Rebecca responded to his greeting with a firm handshake, then glanced at Henry and offered a friendly nod. "Hi, Henry."

At that moment, the guy from the band pushed his way through the crowd to their table. "There's my beautiful bride," he said, sweeping Rebecca into an affectionate hug.

Trisha introduced Colton to Rebecca's husband, Mick, the musician/singer with the band playing tonight and the owner of Mo's.

"Good to meet you, Colton," Mick shook his hand. Then, he told the rest of the group how glad he was they stopped in. "Everything's on the house tonight. My compliments because you got Rebecca out of the office."

"Hey, everyone's here." Rayna appeared next to their booth with a pitcher of beer in each hand. She set them on the table, then hugged Rebecca. "I'm working but, luckily, on a break, so I'll hang with you for a while," she announced cheerfully as she slid into the booth next to Henry.

"Enjoy yourselves tonight. I have to get back to the band. Looks like they're ready to start up again." He kissed Rebecca on the cheek, then headed toward the stage.

Rebecca and Scarlett slid into the booth next to Colton. Rayna passed a pitcher of beer toward Trisha. "You need a refill, and so does Colton. What about you, Rebecca? Are you drinking beer tonight, or do you want me to make you a Butterscotch martini?"

"Beer is fine," Rebecca replied with a smile, reaching for the mug the waitress had left earlier. "You're on a break. Sit down and relax for a few minutes."

Rayna smiled. "Thank you. But only for a minute. We're busy tonight."

"I need a refill," Henry said as he wiped chicken wing sauce off his fingers.

Rayna slid a pitcher toward him. "Help yourself."

The band began to play a song, one of Colton's favorites. "Come dance with me," he whispered to Trisha. She smiled, and his heart melted. He led her onto the crowded dance floor and pulled her close. He found himself swaying gently with Trisha in his arms as the soft strains of a George Strait ballad filled the room. Her head rested lightly on his shoulder, her soft breath grazing his neck, and the sweet scent of her hair enveloping him. He could feel her breasts' steady rise and fall as they pressed against his chest. It was electrifying, sending shivers down his spine, and igniting warmth within his body. The song ended, and Colton leaned in to kiss her.

As their lips touched, Mick shouted from the stage, "Let's rock this place." Immediately, the band unleashed a torrent of heavy metal sound. The crowd erupted into a deafening roar of approval.

Breaking the kiss, Colton shouted above the noise, "This place is wild. Come on, let's get back to the table."

Trisha nodded, grabbed his hand, and followed him closely as they weaved through the maze of people on the dance floor.

Back at the table, they were met with fresh pitchers of beer and some cheerful friends laughing hysterically at something Henry had said. Colton and Trisha were about to take their seats when Rayna announced, "Break's over. You folks have fun, and I'll catch up later." With a casual wave, she headed toward the large horseshoe bar on the opposite side of the room.

As they settled into their seats, Trisha turned to Rebecca, "I heard your law practice is keeping you busy."

She nodded; the weariness was evident in her eyes. "Yes. I've hardly had a moment to myself."

Trisha turned her attention to Colton. "Did I tell you Rebecca is an attorney?"

Trying to keep the mood light, he responded, "Nice to know. Everyone needs a good attorney friend."

Henry chimed in, injecting his sense of humor. "Do we get the friends and family discount?"

Laughter erupted. Scarlett mock punched Henry's arm.

Rebecca joined in the laughter, reassuring them, "Of course."

As the jovial atmosphere settled, Rebecca's cell phone rang. She reached into her handbag, grabbed the phone, and glanced at the screen. "Sorry, I need to take this call."

Scarlett protested, "No, it's after hours."

Rebecca urgently explained, "I have a big case pending, and my assistant is doing some research for me. She may have found something important." She slid from her seat and added, "I'll take this call in Mick's office. Colton, wonderful to meet you." She hurried from their booth, leaving the four of them alone.

"Hey, how about a game of pool? Henry suggested.

Colton glanced at Trisha, "You play?" His hand slid under the table and patted Trisha's knee affectionately.

A mischievous smile danced across Trisha's lips. "Sure. I'm willing if you all are."

"Well, all right." Henry dug into his pocket and pulled out a wad of bills. He scrutinized them momentarily before suggesting, "How's twenty a game, best three out of five? Winner takes all."

Before Colton could respond, Trisha yelled, "You're on!" Her eyes sparkled with competitive zeal.

Finding an empty table, they flipped a quarter for the break. Colton and Trisha won, and the game was set in motion.

As he chalked his cue, he leaned close to Trisha. "Are you any good?"

"Oh, yeah," she purred, the challenge unmistakable in her voice. She angled her head. "We'll be going home with the cash." She punctuated her words with an evil laugh.

"You two ready to play?" Henry asked as he walked up from behind them.

Colton and Trisha exchanged glances and he immediately recognized the light of battle flame in her eyes. She lifted her hand in a high five. "Let's whip these two amateurs."

Colton broke first, sending the cue ball crashing into the racked balls with precision. It was a clean, well-scattered break, sinking two balls into pockets. He went for another and missed.

Henry stepped to the table and sank three balls in short order before losing his turn.

Colton stood back, his eyes fixed on Trisha as she bent over the pool table, her low-slung jeans accentuating every tantalizing curve. She pursed her lips in concentration as she lined up her shots, executing each move with a fluid grace that left him utterly captivated. She rivaled

Henry by getting three balls in before losing her turn.

Scarlett lined up her shot, but it only rolled about three inches when she hit the cue ball. "Rats! I shoulda hit it harder." Her face glowed with embarrassment.

"That's okay," Henry said as he reached out and pulled her into a hug. "You'll do better next time."

Colton chalked his cue and stepped to the table. He was about to take his shot when someone yelled from across the room, "Fight!"

The words barely registered in Colton's mind when a loud crash erupted. People screamed. Someone nearby shoved another guy, knocking over a pool cue rack. The clatter of fallen cues echoed around him. He grabbed Trisha and held her close as chaos exploded.

"Ah, shit!" Henry growled. "Get the girls out of here." He pointed to the back exit sign as he pushed a wide-eyed Scarlett toward Colton.

Trisha pulled away from him and held her cue stick like a baseball bat. She looked ready to jump into the fight. Colton, realizing the danger, grabbed her arm, attempting to get her out of harm's way.

Before he could drag her towards the exit, bar stools were sent flying through the air, bottles shattered against walls, and the band's music abruptly stopped playing. The bar descended into utter pandemonium, with patrons either scattering to avoid the brawl or cheering on the fighters.

Henry charged into the action with fists swinging. Colton watched Henry's first punch connect with a bald, muscular biker, sending the man reeling.

Still holding the cue stick like a weapon, Trisha swung it with determination at an obviously drunk guy who was recklessly hurling pool balls around the room. The stick cracked against a table, causing the shocked drunk to stagger backward.

Cursing under his breath, Colton realized he needed to get Trisha and Scarlett out of there before things got even more out of hand. He scooped up Trisha and, ignoring her protests, headed for the back exit, where Scarlett was already holding the door open.

They burst into the dimly lit parking lot as three police cars with sirens wailing screeched to a stop near Mo's front entrance.

"Are you both okay?" he asked as he glanced at both Trisha and Scarlett.

Trisha, still seething with frustration, replied, "Yeah. Why didn't you let me hit him? He's one of the guys who started the fight."

"Because I didn't want you getting hurt. Or maybe going to jail." He pointed toward the officers who walked several men in handcuffs from Mo's toward their squad cars.

Trisha finally met his eyes and softened her glare. "Well, thanks."

"You're welcome." He took each girl by their arm. "Come on. I'll take you home."

"Hey, do you think Rayna is all right?" Trisha turned to the back door.

Scarlett reassured them. "Rayna's fine. I saw her duck behind the bar. It's not her first rodeo. She knows what to do."

Still processing the wild scene he'd just witnessed, Colton asked, "So you're saying fights often happen at Mo's?"

"Sure. Probably every weekend," Scarlett confirmed.

"Good to know," he muttered as he guided the girls toward his truck.

Chapter Twenty-one

Later that night, Colton lay in bed thinking about Trisha. He'd dropped her at her house after their evening at Mo's. Scarlett was spending the night with her, so as much as he wanted to stay at her place, he'd figured it best he went home. Besides, he had to get to the barn by dawn.

In the darkened bedroom, he let his thoughts drift to places he typically kept hidden away—memories from his high school days, a time that felt like it belonged to a different universe, yet the recollections were vivid and painful. Colton closed his eyes, allowing the past to wash over him like a tidal wave. They'd moved to the city after his dad passed away. Burdened by grief, his mom didn't want to stay on the ranch, so she'd sold everything and bought a townhouse in central Phoenix.

God, it had been hard. Particularly when he'd started at a new school and realized a skinny redneck wouldn't fit in very well. He missed the ranch. He missed the horses, and most of all, he missed his dad.

Then Bobby Thompson entered his life. Colton's lips curved into a wistful smile as he recalled that fateful afternoon. He'd been struggling to fix a stubborn flat tire on his old pickup when a stranger approached him.

"Need any help?" the man had offered.

At first, he'd declined. "I'm good, thanks."

The man glanced at his truck. "Looks like you need a new set of tires."

"Yep. Plan to when I get the money."

"Still in high school?"

"I'm a junior. Hard to find something with hours that fit around school."

After a pause, the man asked, "You know how to groom a horse?"

A surge of excitement coursed through Colton's veins. "I can groom, ride, or break anything you got."

The man had chuckled. "Well," he said, handing Colton a business card, "if you want some hours, show up at the track at six in the morning. I'll put you to work. If it's okay with your parents."

Colton had studied the name on the card and then, meeting the man's eyes with unwavering determination, told him, "I'll be there, Mr. Thompson."

With that promise, a new chapter unfolded in his life, reshaping the essence of his existence.

As it turned out, Bobby Thompson had become more than just a boss. He'd become his mentor and good friend. He'd introduced Colton to the world of Thoroughbred horses, igniting a passion that had given him purpose and direction. After graduation, Bobby had even helped with his college tuition, striking a deal with Colton's mother to ensure a brighter future away from the racetrack. Yet, the nine-to-five world had never felt quite right. He had tried it, but the yearning for the horses had been too strong to ignore. Bobby had welcomed him back with open arms, and all had been well for a while.

Colton let out a heavy sigh, his mind weighed down by the complexity of his emotions. He rolled onto his side, pulling the covers up around his shoulders as if seeking comfort from the impending storm of the past. Regrets clawed at his conscience. Things could have been so different, he mused, but he couldn't rewrite history. All he could do now was find a way to confront the ghosts of the past because he had a sinking feeling that they were about to resurface and haunt him once more.

If he wanted to keep Trisha in his life, the promise to her father had to be broken. And he needed to do it soon before she found out through racetrack gossip.

* * *

Trisha slid out of bed and headed to the kitchen as quietly as possible so she wouldn't wake up Scarlett. She loved her friend dearly, but she had to have some coffee before the fifty questions about her relationship with Colton started. Last night she'd been able to sidetrack Scarlett by joking and laughing about the bar fight at Mo's, but she knew that wouldn't work today.

Her mind began to wander as she poured the hot, comforting liquid into her favorite mug. She thought about the way Colton's eyes crinkled at the corners when he smiled, how he held her hand as he'd walked her to the door last night and the soft kiss they'd shared before he'd said goodnight.

If Scarlett wasn't here, would he have stayed?

Trisha was on her second cup of coffee and had just pushed down the button on the toaster when Scarlett walked in.

"Oh, good, you've made coffee," Scarlett said with a yawn. Her eyes still seemed heavy with sleep.

"Help yourself." She pointed to the cabinet displaying an assortment of coffee cups. "Would you like toast?"

"No thanks. Coffee is all I need." She poured herself a cup and sat across from Trisha at the kitchen table. She took a sip and said, "I can't stay. I have to be in the office this morning for a meeting. But thank you so much for letting me crash here. I couldn't take the chance of a traffic ticket. I'd been drinking too much."

"You're always welcome," Trisha assured her, slathering a generous layer of butter on a slice of toast. "Sure, you don't want some? It's homemade bread."

Scarlett hesitated for a second, then shook her head. "Smells wonderful, but I gotta run." She stood and then placed her empty coffee cup in the sink. "Tell Colton I'm sorry if I ruined your night."

Trisha chuckled, shaking her head, "You didn't ruin anything."

"Seriously. You wouldn't have rather had him here last night than me?" Scarlett laughed, a mischievous glint in her eye.

Trisha's cheeks flushed slightly, and she glanced down at her coffee cup, stirring the contents absentmindedly. The mention of Colton made her heart race, "It's not about one being better than the other, you know. You're my best friend, and I love spending time with you."

Scarlett smiled warmly, her teasing demeanor melting away. "I know, Trisha. I hope you're happy. That's all." She walked from the kitchen.

Trisha rose, walked to the coffee pot, and poured herself another cup.

Five minutes later when Scarlett returned to the kitchen, she was dressed and had combed her hair. "I don't mean to be nosey, but I know you're hesitant about having a relationship with an employee. Lots of people make it work. You can too."

"That's what I keep telling myself." Trisha smiled. "I want to give it a try. It's just scary."

Scarlett offered a smile. "I get it. But Trisha, he really seems like a nice guy."

"I know. He is a nice guy. He says we can make it work. I want to trust him."

"All I can say is follow your heart. Are you seeing him today?" Scarlett asked as she gathered up her purse and cell phone.

"Yes. I'm stopping by the racetrack this morning. I want to check on Icy Tears and see if Colton's found another horse I can buy." She took a breath and then announced, "I've decided to expand my stable."

Scarlett raised an eyebrow. "Wow. You really are getting into this horse racing business."

"I certainly plan to."

"Want to meet up later and talk?" Scarlett asked.

"Sure. Five o'clock at the Ritz?" Trisha proposed.

"I'll be there. I'll call Rayna, too." Scarlett glanced out the window. "My Uber is here." She opened the door and paused.

"I'm looking forward to seeing you both. Bye."

"Bye." Scarlett flashed a warm smile in return, then hurried out, quietly closing the door behind her.

Trisha finished her coffee and then stood. As she loaded the cups into the dishwasher, she thought aloud, "Guess I'd better get moving if I want to get to the racetrack in time to watch the morning workouts."

After a quick shower, Trisha was dressed and driving toward the racetrack. As she drove, her mind wandered to her father. He had walked out on her and her mother when she was only three years old. She couldn't remember much about him except that he had thick brown hair, calloused hands, and a kind face.

Fragments of him came to her mind over the years, but she quickly dismissed them. She'd told herself she wouldn't waste her time remembering someone who didn't care about her. She had always received the same reply from her mother when she'd asked if her daddy was coming home. "Your daddy cares about his horses more than he does us." After a while, Trisha quit asking. It hurt too much to get her mother's harsh reply.

Maybe she should have contacted him and asked him why he'd left. She'd love to hear his answer, but now, it was no longer an option. It was too late. The weight of regret settled in her heart as she gripped the steering wheel tighter. The past still haunted her thoughts as she turned into the parking lot toward the uncertain future with Colton.

Chapter Twenty-Two

Trisha walked into the tack room and found Colton reading a race condition book.

As she entered, he glanced up and smiled. "Good morning, Beautiful." His lips curved into a mischievous smile, "I mean, good morning, Boss Lady."

"I like the beautiful better," she replied with a sly grin. "And I'm great, by the way."

"I'm finding that out."

Ignoring his comment she headed straight to the coffee pot, poured herself a steaming cup, and slid into the chair beside him. "Whatcha reading?"

"Looking at the conditions. Here." He picked up another book and handed it to her.

Trisha accepted the book, her curiosity piqued. She quickly realized it was a sales catalog as she flipped through its pages. The glossy pages held a treasure trove of equine beauties. Her eyes darted up to Colton, ready to ask what she was supposed to do with this when he beat her to the punch.

"The Carter Farm is liquidating their racing stock. See anything you like?" Colton inquired, a note of excitement punctuating his words.

Trisha skimmed through the images of the majestic animals on each page. "Gorgeous horses," she whispered, her voice filled with a sense of awe.

Colton nodded. "Yep. They have some top producers in brood mares, too."

Trisha's thoughts danced toward the future. "Something to think about down the road," she mused, her eyes still fixed on the alluring images. Then, she spotted something that made her heart skip a beat, "Oh, hey, look at this one." She pointed to the grey filly on page fifteen.

Colton smiled as she turned the book toward him. "I noticed her. A two-year-old with good bloodlines, but she'd need a lot of training before she gets to the track."

Trisha's gaze remained locked onto the horse's captivating features, her heart skipping a beat as she admired the photograph. Her thoughts raced with a mix of emotions and aspirations. "Yeah. But look at that face."

Colton chuckled, his voice laced with affection, as he leaned over to study the page. "She's good-looking for sure." He straightened into his chair, his gaze shifting from the catalog to her. "One problem with that horse is she's going to be more than you can afford. But I gotta admit you have a good eye. She's probably the most expensive horse in their racing stock. Maybe you should think about a broodmare instead."

Trisha's heart sank slightly at the mention of affordability. She had been so captivated by the filly's beauty that she had momentarily forgotten the financial constraints of her racing dreams. 'Where in the world would I keep a mare and a foal?"

Colton's eyes met hers, and he replied, "Where do you plan to keep Icy Tears when this meet closes?"

"Closes? You can't keep him here year-round?"

He frowned as he answered, "Nope."

Questions filled her mind with this unexpected hurdle. She'd just assumed the horses stayed there year-round. "So, what did you and my dad do?"

"We hauled them up to his property."

"Seriously? Is there a barn?" Trisha asked, her voice quivering with a mixture of anticipation and surprise. She had heard stories about her father's property but had never seen it herself. The prospect of discovering a barn on the land opened up a world of possibilities.

"You mean you haven't seen it?"

She shook her head. "No. My mom told me he lived in an old RV up there. I planned to put the land up for sale."

"Good Lord." He scratched the back of his neck. "I think we need to take a ride. Are you free this afternoon?"

"I can be. Let me make a phone call."

* * *

Two hours later, they cruised along the 1-17 at seventy miles per hour, talking about everything under the sun. Trisha had this incredible way of switching subjects at the drop of a hat, and Colton couldn't help but feel a warm connection with her. His heart swelled with admiration for her liveliness and charm. He couldn't contain a soft chuckle. This girl might be a lot of things, but boring was not one of them. Trisha was a captivating whirlwind of emotions and stories.

"So, when was the last time you saw your father?" Colton figured it was time to steer the conversation toward Bobby. He knew it wouldn't be long before Trisha unveiled a new portrayal of her dad.

"Actually, I don't remember. I was only three years old when he left us." Trisha's voice quivered slightly. "I remember vague pictures of him, but most of my memories are manifested from what my family told me." She shrugged, her vulnerability on full display and turned her head toward the passenger window.

His heart ached with an overwhelming desire to protect and comfort Trisha as if he could somehow erase the pain etched in her voice. He wanted to make her world brighter, even though he felt clueless about where to begin.

The silence in the car was thick with unspoken emotions, and he silently vowed to be there for her, to navigate the turbulent waters of her past alongside her. But this commitment came with the caveat that she would allow him to do so once he mustered the courage to reveal all the hidden truths about her father and himself. He took a steadying breath. God only knew what she'd say when he exposed the weaknesses and pain they both had carried.

Colton continued to drive for another hour until the vast ranch property opened before them. He turned his truck onto the curving gravel driveway, which led them toward a picturesque ranch house. Its presence immediately captivated, featuring a lengthy covered front porch with a pair of well-worn rocking chairs.

As the truck came to a stop, he noticed Trisha's curiosity got the best of her. She pressed the button to roll down the passenger window, craning her neck to get a better look. "Wow," she exclaimed, her voice mixed with astonishment and skepticism. "Where are we?"

Colton didn't answer. He shifted into Park and switched off the engine.

Trisha shot him a quizzical look. "Why are we stopping here? Do you know the people who own this ranch?"

"Yep," he responded as he opened the truck door.

Trisha's disbelief mirrored in her expression as she gazed at the well-maintained ranch house. "Seriously, Colton. Why are you so mysterious?"

"I'll answer in a minute. Show some patience," he replied with a smile. He met her in front of his truck, took her arm, and guided her gently. "Come on," he urged, leading her toward the house.

They had covered about half the distance when a lean older man emerged from the side of the home. Spotting them, he called out, "Hey, Colton."

"Charlie, good to see you," Colton greeted with warmth.

The man removed his work gloves and extended his hand, giving him a firm shake. "Why didn't you let us know you were coming? Martha would have fixed you dinner," he said, then turned his attention to Trisha. "And who is this lovely lady?"

"This lovely lady is Trisha Thompson. Bobby's daughter."

Charlie's eyes widened. "Trisha Thompson? Well, I'll be dammed." His cheeks reddened, and he stammered, "Sorry, miss. I mean, nice to finally meet you."

The mix of surprise, embarrassment, and genuine warmth in Charlie's reaction made the moment even more memorable. Colton tried to stifle a chuckle, but it was inevitable. He couldn't help himself.

Trisha extended her hand to Charlie and told him it was nice to meet him, also.

The words were barely out of her mouth when a woman hollered from the house. "Charlie, who's out there with you?"

As Charlie glanced toward the woman, Trisha shot Colton a stern look. He grimaced. She was clearly not happy with his secrecy and expected answers soon.

"It's Colton and Miss Thompson, Martha."

Martha responded, "Well, bring them in here."

Charlie turned and gestured toward the house. "You heard her. Let's head in."

Colton followed them into the house, casting a quick glance around. Nothing had changed since his last visit, except this time, no Bobby Thompson filled the space with his jokes and banter about horses and racetrack gossip. It felt oddly strange, yet he found some comfort in the fact that he was here with Trisha. His stomach tightened. He needed to start explaining that this place now belonged to her.

Before he had a chance, Martha grabbed Trisha in a hug. "Oh, you look just like your daddy. It's wonderful to finally meet you. Come on in and have a seat." She directed them to the dining room table, then headed to the kitchen and began filling the coffee pot with water.

As they settled around the large oak dining table. Charlie spoke. "What brings you up here so early? I didn't expect to see you until March."

Colton hesitated, glancing at Trisha, who was clearly overwhelmed and bewildered by the situation. "I wanted Trisha to see the place. She—"

Charlie interrupted. "Oh, of course." He fixed his gaze on Trisha, his eyes radiating with kindness. "So, Miss Thompson, what do you think?"

Trisha's cheeks flushed with what Colton knew was a mixture of emotions, surprise, uncertainty, and probably a touch of embarrassment.

"I think it's very nice," she answered. Her smile displayed a hint of fragility.

Colton sensed her confusion and anxiety growing. She had no idea why she was there or what was expected of her, and it was starting to become embarrassing for both of them. He realized he needed to act quickly. This situation was slipping out of his control.

Martha returned with the pot of coffee, and her presence was a momentary respite. She placed the coffee on the table and retrieved four mugs from the buffet near the large picture window. "Help yourselves," she said with a warm, welcoming smile. She maneuvered around the table and sat at the far end. "If you're hungry, I have muffins down at our house. I could run get them."

"No, Martha, just coffee's fine. But thank you."

As they drank coffee and talked about horses, the atmosphere in the room began to shift from awkward to something more manageable. Charlie wanted to hear the latest news from the track. Colton happily obliged.

"More coffee?" Martha offered.

"No thanks, Martha." Colton stood, making a decisive move to steer the course of their visit. "Actually," he said, "I like to show Trisha the barn." Giving her his best smile, he turned to Trisha and asked, "Would you like to visit the horses?"

Trisha's eyes brightened with evident excitement. "I would love to." She pushed her chair back and expressed her gratitude to Martha, "Thank you for your hospitality. It's very nice to meet you."

Martha beamed a mixture of fondness and sadness. "Your daddy was a dear friend. He'll sure be missed."

"Thank you," Trisha replied, her voice hinting of longing. She joined Colton near the door, which he held open for her.

As they stepped outside, the setting sun cast long, slanting lavender shadows through the towering trees. The air was filled with the earthy scent of pine and freshly mown grass, creating a rustic and nostalgic ambiance somewhere in the background. The low, melodious bellow of a cow resonated, adding to the sense of tranquility, and belonging in this place that was so significant at this moment.

Colton's heart swelled with emotion as they approached the barn. He couldn't contain his curiosity. "What do you think of this place?" he asked, his voice filled with anticipation and a hint of nerves.

She gazed around at the tranquil surroundings before answering. "I think it's beautiful," she began, her tone tinged with confusion and frustration. "I just don't know why we're here. I thought you were taking me to my property. It's going to be dark by the time we get there." Her patience was clearly running thin.

Colton paused, his excitement mingling with a sense of responsibility. He took a deep breath, trying to contain his overwhelming excitement. He blurted, "Trisha, this is your property."

Chapter Twenty-Three

"You're telling me that this ranch belonged to my father?" Trisha's voice trembled with disbelief, and her eyes blazed with a fiery intensity that suggested she thought Colton was lying, playing a trick. Her frustration was unmistakable as she stepped closer, jabbing a pointed finger to his chest. "You're joking, right?"

Colton took a step back, lifting his hands in defense. "No joke, Baby. This place is all yours."

"Mine?" Her voice quivered despite her best efforts. "This can't be right. I was told he was broke. He was a racetrack bum. Living in an old RV." She glared at Colton, her eyes wide and searching for answers, her hope resting on him.

Colton softened his voice, hoping to reassure her. "Honey, that's probably true at some point. But for as long as I knew him, he worked hard, saved his money, made good investments, and built a legacy. One he hoped to share with you. Instead, he left it to you. I only wish he'd lived to show you around."

"You are serious? The land, the house, the barn, the horses are mine?"

He nodded. Then, trying to keep everything honest, he added, "Not the horses. There are two here. One's mine, and the old pony horse is Charlie's. Your dad gave him free boarding."

Trisha's brow furrowed. "Actually, who *are* Charlie and Martha?"

"Charlie works here at the ranch," Colton explained. "Martha's his wife and does some light housekeeping. They live in the guest house out back."

"I can't believe this." Trisha stepped closer and mock-punched his upper arm.

Colton winced, the unexpected force of her actions catching him off guard. "Ouch," he muttered while he rubbed the spot where she'd struck him, pretending it had hurt.

"You jerk. You knew this all the time and didn't tell me."

Realizing he'd gone too far, he stepped back slightly, raising his hand again, this time in a gesture of surrender, trying to calm the storm she was directing toward him. She wasn't finished. She gritted her teeth, her frustration and anger vividly expressed.

"I'm sorry," Colton pleaded. "I thought it would be fun to see your reaction. I didn't mean for you to take offense."

"I *am* offended." She crossed her arms and turned her back to him.

Desperation tinged his voice as he tried to make amends. "I'm really sorry, Trisha. I hoped you'd find it exciting to know this was all yours and see another side of your dad."

He watched her take a deep breath and then look around at the house, the barn, the white fence lining the paddock. He remembered the days when the horses raced around back in that area. If only she could see it all through his eyes.

She turned back to him, and he flinched, worried she might smack him again. Instead, she flung herself into his arms and exclaimed, "I love it!"

* * *

They spent a leisurely half an hour in the barn. Colton's joy at reuniting with his horse, Maverick, was evident, and he introduced him to Trisha with a proud smile. She couldn't help but be enchanted with how he spoke to the horse, a tender connection that melted her heart. She'd also met Lucky, Charlie's quarter horse. Colton shared how Lucky had been one of the best pony horses on the track before Charlie's retirement three years ago. He had brought Lucky to her dad's place to enjoy a peaceful life, letting him do as he pleased after enduring the abuse of the high-strung Thoroughbreds. Colton laughed warmly and affectionately, petting the horse's thick neck, making it clear just how deep his love for the old horse ran.

As they headed back to the house, the golden hues of the evening sky were slowly surrendering to the velvety embrace of night. The first stars began to twinkle overhead, casting a magical spell over the landscape. Trisha couldn't contain her happiness as they reached the front porch, a sense of wonder and gratitude washing over her. Her voice quivered with emotion as she whispered, "I can't believe this is mine." She spoke in awe, reflecting her mixed appreciation and astonishment.

The night air had grown cooler, and she shivered slightly as they reached the front door. She stepped back to let Colton open it, a small gesture that spoke of the new chapter unfolding in her life and her warmth toward the man who had shared this life-altering revelation with her.

"It's all yours, baby. Go on inside." He held the door open.

Trisha stepped into the inviting living room and immediately drew her eyes to the rich hardwood floors that projected a sense of timeless elegance. It surprised her how she hadn't noticed when she'd entered the home earlier. Now that it was hers, she looked at it differently.

In the heart of the room, a plush leather sofa beckoned, perfectly positioned to face a wood-burning stone fireplace. Next to the fireplace, a wrought-iron tray held a neatly stacked bundle of logs. The room exuded a cozy ambiance she hadn't noticed earlier. She pictured herself curled up by the fire with a good book and a cup of hot chocolate, especially if it was spiked with a splash of cherry vodka.

Her eyes continued to roam, taking in the meticulous care that had gone into maintaining this space. Not a speck of dust could be seen, a testament to the diligent efforts she assumed of Martha. And, Trisha realized, both Martha and Charlie were conspicuously absent, leaving her alone in the room with Colton. At this moment, the significance of her inheritance and the newfound connection she shared with Colton truly sank in.

Turning to Colton, her eyes locked with his, her accusation a turbulent mix of confusion and frustration. "You've known about this the entire time, haven't you?"

"I knew you inherited this ranch, yes. But I honestly thought you knew there was a house and barn. I never thought you assumed it was undeveloped land."

"You could have asked." She let out a deep, steadying breath, her emotions simmering just beneath the surface.

Colton shrugged, his voice tone gentle but firm. "Why would I do that? You'd have thought I was getting into your business."

"Still, you could have said something."

She continued to walk around the room, her steps deliberate, her eyes scanning the pictures that adorned the walls. She came across one featuring two men and studied it intently. "Is this my dad, and who's the young guy?" She leaned closer to the photo. "Oh, my goodness, is this you?"

Colton nodded with a hint of nostalgia. "That's me. I was a kid when I first met your dad."

Trisha continued to study the picture, her thoughts racing, "You were cute. High school jock?"

Colton chuckled, shaking his head. "Definitely not."

Even though she was teasing, she couldn't help but wonder what he was like as a teen. She smiled and the tension in the room seemed to ease as they shared a moment of humor amidst the whirlwind of emotions.

"I'm going to check the fridge while you look at the place." Colton headed toward the kitchen, leaving her alone to explore the house.

"Excellent idea." Her voice carried a touch of gratitude as she moved along the hallway, her fingers lightly grazing the pictures adorning the walls. Most photos depicted horses, featuring moments of triumph in the winner's circle at various racetracks. She smiled as she observed her father in different stages of his life, capturing moments that told the story of his passion for horses. He had been a remarkably good-looking younger man, a fact that hadn't escaped her notice. No wonder her mother fell for him.

Then, her attention was captivated by a specific photograph that distinguished itself from the rest. Within it, her father stood alongside a man with a noticeable, familiar face. She squinted, trying to identify him when suddenly, it struck her— a younger James Ledger. It proved to be a fascinating revelation. In the picture, both men wore broad smiles, and it was clear they had spent an enjoyable day together, accompanied by a magnificent Thoroughbred.

"Hey, Colton," she called from the hallway. "Were my dad and Ledger friends?"

As he stepped into the room, his expression turned serious. "More than friends. They were partners."

Her curiosity spiked. "Seriously. So why don't you like him?"

He hesitated for a moment; his gaze distant. "It's a long story. We'll get around to it." He cleared his throat, then obviously not wanting to discuss it further, changed the subject. "Say, do you like chicken? Martha left a plate of fried chicken in the fridge. And I think I saw some potato salad."

Trisha furrowed her eyebrows. She wasn't going to let him get away with vague answers, but with her stomach rumbling at the mention of food, she decided to momentarily put her inquisition on hold.

"Sounds delicious," she said with a nod. Right now, she was ready to eat just about anything.

She followed Colton to the kitchen. "I'll find us something to drink."

She rummaged through the kitchen cabinets and found an unopened bottle of tequila. "What have we got to make a margarita?"

Colton opened the fridge door and stared inside. "There's some lemon-lime soda. Will that work?"

"Works for me. How about you?"

He flashed her a wry smile. "Whatever you make, I'll drink."

Trisha couldn't help but tease. "Brave man."

By the time Colton had plated the fried chicken and potato salad, Trisha had mixed her version of a margarita. They settled into the dining room and started their meal.

The atmosphere was relaxed, and the conversation flowed freely. Trisha was enthralled by the stories Colton shared about the early racing days and the lessons her dad taught him. She was discovering a different side of the man her family had bad-mouthed to her over the years. It was becoming clear to her how much her mother had been hurt by him leaving. She also noticed that James Ledger's name was absent from Colton's stories, a detail that struck her strange since finding out her dad and he had been partners at one time. She knew there must be more to that story, and although she decided to bide her time, the determination to uncover the truth simmered beneath the surface.

With their meal finished, Trisha cleared the dishes. She entered the living room to find Colton placing a log in the fireplace. "I made us fresh drinks."

He turned to her and smiled. She felt goosebumps rise on her arms. Wearing jeans and a red plaid flannel shirt, he looked like a hero in one of her sweet romance movies. She sat on the sofa, kicked off her shoes, and watched as the flames rose in the fireplace, giving the room a soft, warm glow.

Colton sat beside her on the couch and took his drink from her hand; his fingers brushed her as he did. "Remember the last time we sat on a couch?" He sipped his drink and placed the glass on the coffee table. His hand moved to the back of her neck and gently massaged.

"How can I forget." Warmth spread through her system. She closed her eyes and savored his fingers moving up and down her neck.

He leaned closer and whispered near her ear, "Let me show you the room I always stayed in."

Her heart rate quickened, and his breath, warm on her cheek, made her shiver. "It's been a long day. I need a shower," Trisha gently pulled away and swallowed the rest of her margarita.

Colton's eyes flashed a mischievous glint. "I have a better idea."

With an unexpected yet tender strength, Colton swept her off her feet and carried her into the bathroom. He settled her on the edge of a luxurious garden tub, and with a twist of the faucet, he initiated the cascade of water. Steam gradually rose, enveloping them in a warm, soothing hug.

He leaned over her and kissed her softly, then pulled the sweater she wore over her head. After tossing it aside, he reached around and unfastened her bra, letting the lacy garment slide to the floor next to her feet. Her nipples hardened immediately from the damp air filling the small bathroom.

"Honey, you are so beautiful." He spoke as his eyes roamed her body. He leaned close and ran his tongue over each nipple, then lifted his head, and their eyes locked for a second before he pulled her to her feet. Holding her close, he unzipped her jeans, slid them down, then slowly removed them along with her panties. Her body tingled as she watched him stand back and, with swift movements, discard his clothes, tossing them into a pile alongside hers.

She stared at him with tipsy tequila eyes. His chest was lean and firm, shoulders broad, legs muscular, and his manhood left her speechless. Her hand lifted to touch him, but he stepped back with a smile, tilting the corners of his mouth.

"Let's not rush anything." He turned to the linen closet and reached for a bottle. Trisha recognized it immediately as one of her favorite bath salts. She started to ask if Martha had meticulously stocked the bathroom or if her dad had cared for these details, but she decided not to inquire. She realized it was best to let the information remain mysterious.

He returned to the tub and poured a generous amount of fragrant sandalwood and patchouli-scented bath salts into the already brimming water. The bathroom was soon filled with the delightful aroma, an irresistible invitation to unwind and let go of the day's tensions.

He took her hand and helped her step inside, then followed and settled against the back of the tub. Trisha slid backward, fitting easily between his spread legs. She leaned her head against his solid chest and closed her eyes. She felt as if she was floating in a warm sea of silk and bubbles.

It doesn't get any better than this.

Her hands rested on his muscular thighs as his strong hands moved to her breasts. His fingers began circling each nipple, and she felt his hardness press into her back,

"Trisha, let me love you." His words were soft against her ear, but the meaning came through loud and clear. She closed her eyes, relaxed, and savored the moment.

Chapter Twenty-Four

Colton woke to find Trisha's deep brown eyes staring at him. The first light of daybreak streamed through the bedroom window, gently kissing her tousled hair, and she seemed to radiate an almost mystical glow.

"Good morning," she said as she ran her fingers lightly over his chest, igniting a spark that spread from the inside out like a flame in the chill of dawn.

"Good morning." He reached up to stroke her hair, marveling at how the silky strands slipped through his fingers like liquid.

"How did you sleep?" she asked, nuzzling closer to him.

"I slept great." He kissed her gently on the cheek. "I wish we could linger in bed just like this all day. But I need to get back to Phoenix."

The playful pout that formed on her lips tugged at his heart. "Oh, no." She rolled onto her back. "Can't we stay here?"

Colton sighed, a mix of desire and responsibility battling within him. "You can, if you want, but I've got horses to check on.

Moonlit Mirage is running tomorrow." He patted her arm. "And I need to find a race for Icy Tears."

"Yes." She pulled away and sat up. "We do need another race. And now that we have a place to bring them off-season, let's talk about my second horse. Let's check that sale catalog again."

Colton laughed as he slipped from the bed and headed toward the bathroom. He stopped and half-turned to face Trisha. "Hurry and get dressed. We'll grab breakfast on the way."

Thirty minutes later, they were cruising toward Phoenix. Colton finished his breakfast sandwich and took a sip of his coffee as he drove. His gaze occasionally drifted to Trisha. She was reaching the final bites of her sandwich, and he knew once she finished eating the questions would start. Until then, he'd relax and enjoy the peaceful ride.

"So," Trisha said, breaking the silence. "Just how long were Ledger and my dad partners?"

The tranquility was shattered, and a heavy sigh escaped Colton's lips. His hands tightened on the steering wheel as he contemplated how to respond. Trisha's question was like a key with the potential to unlock Pandora's box of long-buried emotions and secrets.

"Three years, I think," Colton responded. "Your dad was in a pretty bad place after his divorce."

"You mean after he left his wife and little girl," Trisha retorted with a note of bitterness.

Colton cleared his throat. "Anyway, afterward, he was broke, living in an old RV. Finally, after some soul-searching, he quit drinking and gambling. He was trying to get his life together."

"Oh, boo friggin' hoo."

"Trisha," he tried to sound firm, "do you want me to tell you what happened?"

Her eyes met his, and she nodded with a sigh. "Yes. Sorry. Go ahead."

He took a breath and continued, his memories resurfacing, revealing the weight of those troubled times. "Your dad was running a couple of horses that he'd claimed. But he wasn't having much luck. He couldn't seem to catch a break." He glanced at Trisha, hoping to see empathy.

Her response was a dismissive eye roll, indicating impatience with her father's past struggles.

"Then along came James Ledger offering a lucrative business proposition. They'd go partners, and Ledger would bankroll the setup. Your dad would train the horses and pay him back at a decent percentage. After settling the original amount, it would be a fifty-fifty business arrangement."

"But if Ledger was a trainer, why would he need my dad to train? Wouldn't he do it all himself?"

Colton clarified, "He was a breeder. He was primarily involved in raising Arabians, stunning show horses worth thousands. But he had a gambling issue and was becoming increasingly drawn to the Thoroughbred racing end of the business. The difference between him and your dad was that Ledger didn't care about the money. He had plenty and was willing to gamble it. He knew your dad was a good horseman and he could pay big bucks for a capable trainer."

Trisha nodded, seeming to absorb the details. "Okay. So why didn't they remain partners?"

"Ledger had some very wealthy acquaintances that he'd persuaded to invest in Thoroughbreds. Anyone in the industry will tell you that horse racing is a gamble. Countless things can go wrong. And they did. Especially when Ledger was using a large portion of the win money to support his gambling. The owners were losing money at an alarming rate. They began pressuring Ledger for their invested share back."

Trisha's eyes widened with curiosity. "Are we talking about a lot of money?"

"Thousands," Colton admitted, his voice heavy with the gravity of the situation. "By then, Ledger had watched most of his wealth vanish, devoured by the expenses of keeping his Arabians along with the

Thoroughbreds and his gambling habits. The walls were closing in on him. He got desperate."

"What did my dad think of all this?"

"He didn't know. Your dad wasn't privy to the grim financial reality. Ledger kept him in the dark where money was concerned. Your dad trusted him to handle all their finances."

"So, what happened?"

"Ledger concocted a scheme to bail himself out. His horses were heavily insured. Ledger planned to have one stolen and collect the insurance money."

"That's...that's horrible."

Colton nodded somberly and blew out a breath, his thoughts haunted by the memories of that day. "Yeah. The worst part is I was at the racetrack, cleaning out a stall. Ledger didn't realize I was there, and I overheard him arranging the theft. When he saw me, he threatened me. He told me that if I ever breathed a word of what I'd heard, he'd make it look like your dad was the one behind it." Colton released a deep breath. "I was young, intimidated, paralyzed with fear, so I kept quiet."

Trisha's expression twisted with a mix of anger and empathy. "Geesh. You must have been terrified."

Colton's voice quivered slightly as he continued. "Yeah, I was, but that's no excuse. My conscience ate at me, and I finally worked up the courage to tell your dad. As you can imagine, he confronted Ledger, and that's when everything went from bad to worse."

"What could possibly make it worse?"

"Ledger said he had evidence to frame him for the entire scheme. He would ruin your dad's reputation, strip him of his trainer's license, and maybe send him to jail. And then he brought up your family and mentioned how he'd hate to see anything happen to his lovely ex-wife and little girl. Your dad got the message loud and clear."

Trisha's eyes widened in disbelief. "How can he still be around after all that?"

"He's got connections. Once everyone got their share of the insurance money, they forgave his sins. Then, the old man Ledger passed away, leaving his only son, James, with millions. He inherited the family fortune, sold the remaining Arabians, bought some good breeding stock, and started up his own stable of Thoroughbreds. With the money to buy good horses, he was back on top before long."

Trisha grimaced. "What a despicable person."

"Meanwhile," Colton continued, "your dad worked hard and repaid all the original set-up fees he owed. Once that debt was settled, he cut off all communication. But Ledger has always harbored bitterness."

"Why? If Dad repaid him the start-up money and kept his mouth shut, why care?"

"Ego. Your dad was the only man Ledger couldn't buy or bend to his will. That's something he can't let go of."

* * *

Trisha sat in silence, absorbing everything Colton had shared. She leaned back against the passenger seat headrest, closed her eyes, and let her thoughts race through her mind. Finally, she turned to Colton. He was staring straight ahead at the road. A muscle worked in his jaw.

"Colton, you know nothing was your fault. You can't keep blaming yourself."

His voice quivered slightly as he responded. "I was a wimp, Trisha. I should have spoken up. Instead, I kept my mouth shut and let Ledger dangle that empty threat over your dad's head. I was a coward."

Trisha offered compassionate reassurance. "You were young, not a coward."

Colton continued to stare straight ahead, never glancing her way. "I wasn't raised like that, Trisha. I was brought up to do the right thing. If my father were here, he'd be ashamed of me."

"Or," Trisha countered, "he'd be proud of you for eventually telling my dad."

Colton's self-reproach persisted. "I dropped the ball. I let Ledger get away with theft. I looked the other way and allowed him to collect the insurance money. That, to me, is the very definition of being a coward."

"Promise me you'll stop blaming yourself. I'm sure my dad never did."

"Your dad was an incredibly forgiving man," Colton acknowledged. "I never heard him speak ill of anyone, even Ledger. I'm sure he despised him, but he never verbalized it. He believed that everyone had to confront their own demons eventually. It wasn't for him to pass judgment, only to strive to do his best. But that was wrong. We both should have spoken up."

Trisha considered the situation for a minute. Then she asked, "Do you think you should turn him in now?"

Colton's expression darkened as he shook his head. "Nothing would come of it. There's no evidence besides my word, and too many years have passed. Besides, he'd involve your dad and tarnish his good name. Since he isn't here to defend himself, I won't take that chance."

Trisha reached over and patted his arm. "I appreciate that."

They didn't speak for the next twenty-five miles. Each caught up in their own thoughts.

Chapter Twenty-Five

Moonlit Mirage was running in a maiden race, her first time competing against other horses her age. Colton appeared nervous as he and Trisha walked the spirited filly towards the paddock. Upon reaching the entrance, he handed the lead rope to José and then, taking Trisha's hand, moved to the side to observe. As they watched, the paddock judge called out the filly's name as she was led past them. Once José had her safely in the saddling stall, the judge verified her identity by checking her tattoo. Then, the saddling process began.

In the adjacent stall, another filly started throwing a mini fit, rearing and leaping as the saddle blanket was placed on her back. This commotion caused Moonlit Mirage to toss her head and press her body against José. It took some effort, but he finally managed to calm her enough to complete the tack-up process.

B.J. emerged from the jockey's room wearing Colton's stable's orange and white silks. He strolled out with an air of confidence, casually adjusting his shirt sleeves as his gaze swept across the paddock.

Spotting Colton and Trisha, a smile spread across his tanned face. He waved and made his way over to them.

"Remember, don't let her get away from you," Colton emphasized with conviction.

"Yes, sir," he responded respectfully.

They exchanged a handshake, and Colton told the jockey, "Safe ride."

Nodding in acknowledgment, B.J. turned to take Trisha's hand. She offered him a firm shake, then watched him head toward the stall where Moonlit Mirage waited.

"Riders up," the paddock judge announced, prompting the jockeys to be given a leg up into their saddles and head toward the starting gate. As the excitement built, Trisha grasped Colton's arm. Together, they positioned themselves near the rail, their favorite spot for watching the races.

Craning her neck to see Moonlit Mirage, Trisha found her just as she was being loaded into the starting gate. Thankfully, she went in easily. However, the horse next to her balked, and it took several attempts before the track crew finally got her loaded. Meanwhile, Colton's entry appeared to be growing increasingly restless.

"Come on, get in there," Colton exclaimed, giving the rail an impatient rap with a rolled-up racing form. "That horse is making Moonlit Mirage nervous."

Trisha understood his apprehension. In any horse race, the unexpected could happen, but with first-time horses, the odds of something going wrong felt even more frightening.

Finally, the horses were all securely loaded into the starting gate.

The bell rang. "And they're off!"

Moonlit Mirage broke well and surged forward, taking up the fourth position in the compact group of six horses. Through the first turn, she maintained her place, and Trisha held her breath, her eyes fixed on the colorful silks the jockey wore.

Coming down the stretch, Moonlit Mirage loomed up on the horse in front of her to place third at the wire.

"Is third good for a first time?" Trisha asked when the race was final.

"Yeah, she just got tired. We'll get a win next time." Colton reached for her hand. "Come on. We've got a horse to bathe and feed."

Trisha nodded and fell in step with Colton as he headed to catch B.J. and hear his thoughts about the race.

* * *

Back at the barn, Colton and José bathed Moonlit Mirage, dried her off, and put her on the walker for thirty minutes before taking her inside to feed. Once Colton was confident that she'd come back from the race in top form, he entrusted the remaining process to José.

He found Trisha in his office, engrossed in a game on her phone. She looked up, her face brightening with a smile.

"Feeling hungry?" he inquired, hoping she was because he was starving.

"I'm always hungry. What sounds good to you?" She dropped her phone into her purse and locked eyes with him.

"What do you say to Chinese take-out? I'm beat and in bad need of a shower. I probably smell like a goat."

"Sounds perfect."

"Great. Let's head out."

As they left Colton's office, Trisha gave him an appreciative smile and his hand a gentle squeeze. At that moment, he felt his heart lift. Yeah, with Trisha, maybe he could leave his past mistakes behind and make their relationship work.

Forty-five minutes later, they'd swung by Trisha's condo, where she quickly retrieved a change of clothes, then made a stop at a fast-food restaurant, and now were at his house. He told Trisha to make herself at home while he grabbed a quick shower.

Emerging from the bathroom, he discovered her sitting in front of the TV. The food containers were neatly arranged on the coffee table, all ready to be devoured. She'd even found a bottle of wine and had poured each of them a glass.

Impressed, he blurted, "I knew I loved you for some reason." As the reality of his words hit, he stammered, "I mean, you're a woman after my own heart." *I'm behaving like a complete fool.* He took a seat on the opposite end of the couch and reached for a plate.

"Smells good," He scooted closer to her.

She leaned toward him and inhaled deeply. "You smell pretty good yourself."

"Thanks. Just like a forest in the springtime," he teased.

She laughed as she picked up a container and spooned a hearty portion of shrimp and noodles onto his plate.

The conversation was sparse as they hungrily dug into their meal.

After finishing eating and cleaning up their mess, they both settled back on the couch.

"I think we have a race for Icy Tears coming up." He reached for her hand. "It's a claiming race. You need to be comfortable with that."

Trisha's eyes showed a hint of concern. She sat staring straight ahead. Finally, she turned to him, "Explain again to me what a claiming race is."

"It means your horse can be bought. Money is put up ahead of the race on the horse you want. At the end of the race, regardless of the position, the horse is yours.

Of course, money won during the race goes to the original owner."

She sat staring straight ahead. Finally, she turned to him. "If you're sure he won't get claimed."

Colton sighed, his grip on her hand tightening. "You take that chance when you run in a claiming race. But he's got to run if he's going to be a successful racehorse."

"I suppose you're right."

"It's part of the business. Your horse gets claimed, then you take the money and get another one."

Her eyebrows knitted.

"I can't promise he won't get claimed, but no one's been inquiring about him."

"If you think it's a good idea, then fine. Let's enter him."

"Okay." He pulled her closer and kissed her cheek. "Let's go lay down. It's been a long day, and I'm whipped."

"No place I'd rather be than in your bed."

"Oh, lady, what am I going to do with you?" He shook his head slowly as his eyebrows raised.

Smiling seductively, she tossed her head, sending her dark tresses bouncing over her shoulders. "Come on, and I'll show you." She stood and pulled him to his feet.

Laughing, Colton scooped her up and kissed her softly, then whispered, "I have something to show you, too."

Chapter Twenty-Six

Colton's initial task this morning was to work the filly, Patty's Red Royale. Although his stable's workout rider, Bree, referred to her as simply "Queenie" due to her temperament. She was a sweetheart but ran only if she was in the mood. No matter what the jockey did, she crossed the line last. No heart, none, zip, nada. It was becoming impossible to find a jockey willing to ride her.

"What's your plan for her?" Bree inquired as she secured the filly to the hotwalker for a cool down. Not that the horse had exerted herself enough to work up a sweat.

Colton raked his hand through his hair and exhaled a deep breath. "Aw, shit, I intend to call her owner and suggest selling her. She's just not cut out to be a racehorse."

Bree nodded in agreement. "She'll make someone a wonderful pleasure horse. She's very gentle." She wished Colton luck as she grabbed her equipment and headed toward the stalls.

With a heavy heart, Colton knew making the call was necessary, and even though it meant losing a horse from his stable he needed to be honest with the owner. Signaling José to attend to the filly, he headed toward his office. A few minutes later, he'd left a message for Patty's Red Royale's owner and was now focused on organizing the rest of the week's schedule.

Thirty minutes later, he closed his computer, leaned back in his chair, and let his mind drift to last night. He envisioned Trisha's beautiful face, her silky hair cascading over her creamy shoulders. The image of her brought a smile. Oh, yeah, he considered himself a lucky guy. However, as much as he'd like to continue reminiscing about the previous evening, he needed to concentrate on his work at hand.

Finished with the bookwork for today, Colton was about to mosey up to watch Icy Tears workout when his cell phone rang. Checking the caller ID, he noticed it was the horse owner returning his call.

He was far from pleased with Colton's assessment of the filly, and their discussion grew heated. However, after some back and forth, with Colton holding his position, the owner reluctantly agreed. Colton explained that selling Patty's Red Royale would allow them to reinvest the proceeds in a horse with a more promising track record, one with the potential to bring in decent earnings.

After further deliberation, they eventually reached a mutual agreement that this was the best course of action. Colton assured the owner he would handle all the necessary sale arrangements and strive to secure the best possible price. With a sigh of relief, he disconnected the call and headed to the workout track.

Colton arrived at the track with impeccable timing just as Icy Tears began his workout. Bree had the big horse under control, and his breeze went beautifully. Satisfied, he headed to the racing office to enter Icy Tears in an upcoming race.

* * *

The entire day, Trisha tried to focus on the work project due by the month's end. However, memories of being with Colton kept interrupting, and not only was Colton occupying her thoughts, but the ranch house kept entering her mind. She was becoming obsessed with the idea of redecorating. She had begun envisioning transforming the place, upgrading the kitchen with all new appliances. She daydreamed about expanding the kitchen island, contemplating the addition of some stylish wrought iron stools she'd seen while shopping recently. Painting the house inside and out was also on her mental to-do list. Trisha even considered the idea of hiring an interior decorator to provide suggestions for the house's transformation. Of course, she had to watch her budget, especially if she planned to add more horses to her stable.

Forcing herself back to her employment project, she started to work. Her head was buried in her computer when she heard the front door open. She listened to Colton's familiar booted footsteps in the kitchen, then down the hall, and finally to the room where she sat.

She turned to the doorway, and there he stood, holding a bouquet of flowers.

Her eyes widened in surprise. "For me?" she asked.

"For the prettiest Boss Lady I know. So yes, for you." He placed them on the desk, then moved behind her to kiss her cheek while letting his hands rest on her shoulders.

"They're beautiful. Thank you."

"I stopped to pick up some steaks and saw these by the cashier's station. I couldn't resist." He started massaging her shoulders, his strong hands pressing just the right places to ease the tension built up from sitting at the desk all day.

Trisha leaned back and let out a sigh. "Ohhh, that feels so good."

"Hitting the right spot, am I?" His thumb pressed the tight muscles of her shoulders, making her sigh again.

"Just right," she replied.

"I like coming home and having you here." He helped her from the chair and pulled her into him.

"I like being here when—" That was all she got out before his mouth crushed hers.

Heat slid through her as she kissed him back, opening her lips so his tongue could delve deep inside to tangle with hers. He grabbed her waist with one hand and held the back of her neck with the other. They kissed for several minutes before breaking for air.

"God, Trisha, what you do to me," he said, his breath soft against her cheek.

"You do things to me, too." She leaned her head against his chest, listening to the beat of his heart. Inhaling his scent, her eyes slowly closed with satisfaction at being held by him.

"So, what do you want to do now?" he asked quietly.

"Did you say you bought steaks?" She opened her eyes and glanced up to see him grinning.

"I did. Are you hungry?"

"I'm starving."

Taking her hand, he said, "Come on. I'll go light the grill."

Chapter Twenty-Seven

Saturday in the fifth race.

"Riders up!" the paddock judge announced. His words filled the area with electric energy as all the jockeys readied themselves for the impending competition.

Colton's heart raced as he fixated on the scene before him. Icy Tears tossed his head upward, shaking his mane and stamping one front foot. A frown furrowed his brows as he watched nervously while B.J. was given a leg up and then led from the saddling area.

"See you in the winner's circle," Trisha shouted as José turned the horse and jockey to the waiting pony girl who would lead Icy Tears and BJ onto the track and then parade them toward the starting gate.

"He's ready to run. We should get a good race." Colton squeezed Trisha's hand. "See how anxious he is? I sure hope B.J. can hold him in place. We don't want him to tire out too quickly and let horses get by him."

Colton kept his gaze focused on Icy Tears, who couldn't seem to contain his fired-up Thoroughbred spirit. He nipped at the pony horse's neck, revealing the restless anticipation that was coursing through his veins. The pony girl swatted his nose, signaling him to behave himself. It seemed to work. His exuberance momentarily reined in, they cantered toward the starting gate.

"Why is he acting up?" Trisha asked.

"It's normal. He's excited, that's all. B.J. and the pony girl have him under control."

"I'm so worried." Trisha looked at him as she chewed her bottom lip. Concern clearly showing in her eyes.

"Everything's fine." He assured her as he took her hand, giving it a gentle squeeze.

They stepped close to the rail and watched in silent anticipation as the spectators around them whooped and hollered.

Finally, the horses were all loaded. The bell rang, and the gate flew open.

Icy Tears broke well, as usual, and immediately took the lead. But coming out of the first turn, Ledger's entry overtook him. Icy Tears remained in second for the rest of the race. By the time it was all over, both Colton and Trisha were hoarse from yelling.

"They came back safe, and we'll get a good paycheck. That's good, right?" Trisha asked, her voice sounding hopeful.

"That's good for sure." Smiling, he took her hand and guided her toward the paddock where B.J. was unsaddling Icy Tears. Suddenly, Colton's blood ran cold. He watched in horror as a young, unfamiliar man walked to the horse and clipped a shank to his halter. José stepped back with his eyes focused on the ground. His shoulders slumped.

No, no, no! This isn't happening. No one showed interest in taking him.

Colton knew this was a risk you took running in a claiming race, but there was an understanding between trainers. You didn't take a horse just to take it; they'd usually let you know if they had any interest. Which hadn't happened. Besides, everyone around the track knew what this horse meant to Trisha.

"What's wrong? You have a strange look on your face." Her eyebrows knitted in question.

"He got claimed, Trisha." Colton's voice was heavy with sorrow as he delivered the gut-wrenching news.

Trisha's face drained of color.

Colton put his arm around her, pulling her to him in a desperate attempt to console her, but it didn't work. Her body stiffened under his touch, and she jerked herself free, the pain of what happened obviously too much.

"I've lost him?" her voice sounded strained, breaking Colton's heart.

Guilt gnawed at Colton, and he raked a hand through his hair as he berated himself. *I should never have put Icy Tears in this race.*

Trisha's eyes flashed with a pleading, desperate look. "You don't mean it."

"I wish I didn't." He admitted as his voice cracked with his pain. His hands fisted at his sides, and he held his breath as José approached with a paper in his hand. Colton recognized it immediately as the claiming slip. He snatched it, and the words on the paper blurred for a second as the total weight of what happened sank in, crushing him with its devastating reality. "Damn it to Hell. It had to be him."

* * *

Trisha watched through tear-glazed eyes as her horse was led away. "Who took him?" She tugged on Colton's arm, forcing him to look at her. "Who, Colton? Tell me."

"James Ledger."

As the familiar name registered in her brain, her tears dried, and heated anger replaced her grief. "That miserable low down dirty skunk. He has eight horses running here. He doesn't need mine."

"He absolutely doesn't. I'll pay the man a visit."

She squared her shoulder and gritted her teeth, her determination unwavering. "He did this out of spite, Colton."

"I'm *sure* he did," Colton acknowledged. "Leave it to me. I'll make it clear that he knows how you feel."

"After me. I'm going to break his face." She started to follow Icy Tears back to Ledger's stable.

"Trisha, no." He grabbed her arm, forcing her to turn and face him. "I can't let you do something you may regret later."

She looked Colton straight in the eyes. "There won't be any regret. Let me go." She pulled her arm free from his grasp. "Don't even try to stop me."

At that moment, Scarlett and Rayna ran up next to them.

"What's going on?" Scarlett questioned.

"Ledger took my horse. That's what. And I'm going to break that scumbag's nose."

A worried look passed between Scarlett and Rayna.

With a solemn nod, Colton confirmed Trisha's words. The weight of the situation hung heavy in the air.

Both Scarlett and Rayna wrapped their arms around their friend. Trisha fought to control her temper as her heart still pounded. "It's true, my horse is gone."

"Oh, Trisha, I'm so sorry." Rayna offered an earnest apology as she hugged her tight.

But her friend's sympathy did little to alter the fact she no longer owned the horse her father had generously willed to her. Trisha inhaled deeply in an attempt to calm her raging nerves.

"Come on, Trisha," Scarlett urged, her voice soothing. "Let's go get a drink and talk about what you can do."

"Yes," Rayna agreed as she took Trisha's arm. "We'll figure this out."

Reluctantly Trisha nodded. She looked at Colton, who stood next to her with a grim expression on his face.

"I'll see you up in the clubhouse shortly," he assured her.

Trisha turned away and, with each girlfriend holding her firmly, headed toward the clubhouse. She was halfway there when the person she despised with a burning intensity stepped into view. Breaking free of her friends, she confronted him. "You have some nerve, Ledger."

"Why, Trisha, whatever do you mean?" A smug smile creased the corners of his mouth. "I got that horse fair and square in the race *you* put him in."

"You know I needed that race. And you *know* I didn't want to lose him."

"Hey, you want to play with the big boys, better learn the rules." Ledger began to laugh callously.

"I know the rules. I also know a two-faced snake when I see one."

"Trisha, this is a business." The man leaned closer and sneered, his whiskey-tainted breath touching her cheek as he whispered, "If you want a pet, go get yourself a dog, or is that what Colton's for?"

At that remark, Trisha couldn't hold back her fury any longer. She balled her fist and delivered a powerful punch to Ledger's nose. Blood sprayed, and he staggered backward. Trisha didn't hesitate, she hit him again, this time in the gut. Ledger folded over, clutching his stomach in agony. She lunged forward, planning to tackle him to the ground, but was stopped when Colton grabbed her around the waist and held her back.

"Let me go!" she screamed.

"No. Stop Trisha. He's not worth it." He crushed her to him, Colton's strong arms folded tight around her as her screams eventually turned to sobs. "It's okay, Baby," he whispered against her ear. "I'll fix this. I promise."

Chapter Twenty-Eight

"Are you serious?" James Ledger stated, his voice dripping with disbelief. He coolly eyed Colton as he removed his sunglasses; both eyes had turned purple, and his nose was visibly swollen and bruised where Trisha's fist had connected. The air in Ledger's tack room crackled with tension.

"You heard me. What's your price for me to buy him?" Colton stated, his fingers working the tight knots forming at the back of his neck. He couldn't deny the mounting unease as he pondered the consequences of this high-stakes conversation. He'd like nothing better than to finish what Trisha started but knew it wouldn't get him what he needed. He needed Icy Tears.

Ledger moved to his desk, opened a drawer, and pulled out a bottle of whiskey. He poured himself a small glass and then offered one to Colton.

"No thanks." Colton had no desire to have a drink with the man. He was only here because of Trisha. He'd made her a promise he'd get her horse back, and this was one promise he intended to keep. One way or another.

"Suit yourself." Ledger drained the glass, then cocked his head. "You want to buy Icy Tears from me after running him in a claiming race. What a joke you are, Colton." His voice carried a hint of amusement, but his sharp gaze remained focused on his opponent.

Colton narrowed his eyes on the man and demanded, "Give me a price."

"You're out of your mind," Ledger retorted, his tone now laced with arrogance. "Sure, I'll give you a price. Fifty grand and he's yours."

"We're not talking about a Kentucky-bred Derby contender. He's a forty-five-hundred-dollar claimer."

"Maybe that's true, but I'm growing quite fond of him," Ledger replied, a calculating gleam sparkling in his eyes. "You wanted a price, now you have it."

Colton clenched his jaw, frustration bubbling beneath the surface. "You know I don't have that kind of money."

"Sorry to hear," Ledger said with a sly smile. Then, with feigned reluctance, he added, "I'll tell you what, Colton, since I like you, I'll take forty-five thousand." He stood and his hands flattened on his desktop. "That's my final offer, so better take it before I change my mind."

The room seemed to tighten around him. "I should have gone to the authorities."

"What are you talking about Colton? Are you suggesting I've done something wrong?"

"You know exactly what I'm talking about. Insurance fraud."

"That's a huge accusation," Ledger replied, his voice now colder and more calculated. "I'd be careful what you imply."

"I know what you did."

"I did nothing. That theft was investigated, and the insurance company found me in the clear. I was the innocent victim. I lost a good horse."

"And we both know the insurance company didn't have all the facts." His words hung in the air like a blade cutting through the pretense of civility, and the tension in the small room ratcheted up a level.

"Oh, give me a break!" Ledger straightened. "Get out of here before I decide to press assault charges against your girlfriend." Then added, "don't come back unless you've got cash."

Colton fought the urge to pull the man across his desk and beat him to a pulp. But he knew better. Gritting his teeth, he turned and stomped out of the tack room. However, not before assuring Ledger he'd be back.

* * *

I'm not hurting. I'm doing all right. After all, this is a business, and I can always find another horse.

But it wouldn't be the one her daddy gifted her.

"I'm just not suited for the world of racing. I get too attached to the horses." Trisha raised her margarita to her lips and took a sip. Then, with a deep, contemplative exhale, she peered over the rim of her glass to lock eyes with Scarlett and Rayna. She could sense the sympathy in their expressions, and it was reassuring to know they cared. Nevertheless, it didn't ease her heartache. She drained the margarita glass in one long gulp.

"Don't rush into any decisions," Scarlett offered her advice.

Rayna extended her hand across the table, comforting Trisha with her touch. "Sweetie, things will look brighter tomorrow."

Trisha attempted a smile, appreciating their support, yet she knew she'd never get over her loss of Icy Tears.

"Besides," Scarlett continued, "what would you rather do? Have you considered any options?"

Trisha sighed, her thoughts a tangled mess. "I have no idea. I just know I need to refocus and get back on track, and I don't mean the racetrack. My PR job is suffering because I've been devoting too much time to this stupid horse business."

Rayna inquired, tipping her head slightly. "What about Colton? Do you still see a future with him?"

Uncertainty gripped Trisha as she pondered her relationship with Colton. "I don't even know. I'm confused. I know Colton was only doing his job entering Icy Tears in the claiming race. He made it clear to me the chance we were taking, and I agreed. I never imagined I'd be so upset over losing my horse. And I know it's because Ledger was the one who took him. He did it for spite, not because he saw potential in the horse."

Scarlett and Rayna both exchanged sad looks.

"Mom may have had some valid points about the lifestyle. Not everyone can fit into this world. I don't know if I'm strong enough. Maybe I should take a step back from everything. Colton included."

Scarlett weighed in with concern. "You need to really think it through before walking away from a nice guy."

"Well, I know one thing for sure. Trisha has a dynamite left hook." Rayna burst out laughing.

"No kidding. You punched that jerk Ledger good," Scarlett agreed.

"He deserved it. And if Colton hadn't stopped me, I'd have done some real damage to him." Trisha held up her hand, showing them her swollen knuckles. "Still hurts but worth it."

Rayna's voice cut through the somber air, a spark of spontaneity igniting in her eyes. "You know what we need? A night out like the good old days before Rebecca got married.”

Scarlett chimed in, “Yes. Let’s explore some fun places, meet new people, and just forget about everything for the night. Start fresh tomorrow. What do you say, Trisha? Are you in?”

She hesitated, then answered, “I’ll think about it.”

Rayna leaned forward, her tone pleading. “We can go to some swanky bar in Scottsdale. Listen to a killer band and drink a fancy cocktail. I promise you’ll feel better.”

Trisha sighed, grappling with her conflicting emotions. “I suppose. But I’m not in a party mood.”

“It’s better than going home and drowning in your thoughts about what happened today,” Rayna shot back with determination.

“Going out is definitely a good idea,” Scarlett added, her concern evident. “You need to be around people now, not sitting home alone.”

“Maybe.” The prospect of facing Colton again weighed heavy on her heart. Trisha couldn’t pretend everything was okay just to ease his guilt. A night out seemed like the right diversion, a chance to breathe and take her life in a different direction.

Trisha pulled out her phone and purposefully composed a text to Colton. Her emotions translated into each tap. She read the message aloud. “I need time alone to sort things out. It's best we don't talk for a few days." She looked toward her friends, "how does that sound?"

"Works for me." Scarlett and Rayna both agreed at the same time.

"He'll understand." Scarlett reached over and patted Trisha's hand.

Taking a deep breath, Trisha hit send.

The decision made, Trisha felt a flicker of anticipation, a mix of nerves and excitement swirling in her chest as she prepared to step into the unknown, leaving the echoes of her troubles behind for just one night. "Okay. Let's go get dressed."

Chapter Twenty-Nine

It was nine thirty when Trisha and her friends wandered into the old town Scottsdale bar. An electrifying hum of anticipation hung in the air, and immediately, Trisha felt a surge of energy course through her veins. Her choice of attire was a pair of hip-hugging jeans and a low-cut lacy top that added a touch of allure. Silver high-heeled sandals completed the ensemble, a subtle declaration of her readiness for whatever the night might bring.

Tonight, Trisha resolved to escape the lingering shadows of the loss of Icy Tears and, maybe even Colton. A dance, perhaps, or the company of a charming stranger could provide the perfect distraction, if only for the night. And if not, the camaraderie of her girlfriends promised a delightful evening of laughter and shared moments.

As they stepped into the vibrant bar atmosphere, the thumping music enveloped them, setting the stage for a typical Saturday night. The lively crowd reveled in the pulsating beats, their collective happiness resonating through the venue.

As they headed to a table, Trisha couldn't help but notice the subtle turns of heads and the glances from intrigued guys. It was a familiar response to their entrance, an acknowledgment of the magnetic presence they brought to any establishment. The fact brought a smile.

Once seated they all smiled at each other.

"Cocktail time," Scarlett said, shaking her head happily, her auburn curls dancing around her shoulders.

"First rounds on me tonight, ladies. Let's spend this paycheck from Mo's." Rayna laughed as she raised her perfectly arched eyebrows.

"Excellent," Trisha replied.

Scarlett leaned forward, her expression earnest. "Remember, Trisha you're here to have a good time."

Trisha nodded. "I know. But I don't want to put a damper on your night. Both of you have fun. I'll be fine."

A look passed between Scarlett and Rayna.

"Hey, do I look like a woman with a broken heart?" Trisha asked, gesturing toward herself.

Scarlett quickly answered. "No. As always you look fabulous. I love that outfit."

Rayna nodded in agreement.

Grateful, Trisha acknowledged the compliment, "Thank you." Then, with a smile, she teasingly added, "I want both of you to keep an eye out for Mr. Right. Who knows maybe it's your lucky night."

"What about you?" Scarlett asked. "Are you still looking?"

"Nope. I'm done with men for a while. It never seems to work out for me. I'm always the big loser when I get involved with a man. One way or another."

Scarlett and Rayna exchanged a sobering look between themselves.

"It's okay. Don't let me dampen your fun. I'll be fine. I always am."

Scarlett reached over and patted Trisha's arm while Rayna signaled to their waitress that they were ready to order.

As their drink orders were placed, Trisha discreetly scoped out the room. The adjacent table was filled with a group of four men and two women. They were laughing about something she couldn't overhear. Not that she cared. She had no desire to meet anyone; all she wanted was a memorable evening where her worries could be temporarily set aside in favor of laughter, dancing, and the thrill of the unexpected. If nothing else, she'd know she'd done her best to arrange a distraction from her misery.

Trisha had taken two sips from her margarita glass when a male voice interrupted her thoughts. "Enjoying the night so far?"

She looked up to see a nice-looking man, with light brown hair falling enticingly over his forehead leaning close to their table.

His gaze roamed the table briefly before his gaze settled on Scarlett, unmistakably captivated by her beauty. Seizing the moment, Scarlett invited the man, introduced as Sam, to join them.

Sam seemed nice enough, and Scarlett certainly appeared to think so. Before long, they were on the dance floor, leaving Trisha and Rayna alone.

With the clink of glasses and lively conversation, time passed quickly. Trisha and Rayna shared tales of their past bar escapades, reminiscing about the nights they dressed in disguises and went to different bars, including a Goth bar. Even though it brought up memories of her last failed relationship, Trisha found herself actually having a good time.

"Remember the first time we went to Mo's?" Trisha mused.

Rayna snorted with laughter. "Do I ever. Thanks to my cousin, we witnessed our first bar fight."

"Hey, it worked out great for Rebecca." Trisha lifted her dark eyebrows.

Rayna, still smiling, answered, "That it did. We should all be so lucky. Mick's great."

As the night progressed, Rayna steered the conversation back to the present. "So, Trisha, what are your plans?"

She released a long sigh. "I'm not sure. I think I'll take some time off and go to the property up north. Do some remodeling. Maybe sell it.”

“Didn’t you say there’s a nice couple living in the guest house? What about them?”

“Charlie and Martha. Yes, I have lots to consider.” She slowly stirred her margarita. “I’m just miserable over losing Icy Tears. I’m mad at Colton because he put him in that race, even though it was a joint decision. Heck, I was planning to claim one from another owner. I’m confused. I’m depressed. I don’t know if I can be with Colton without remembering the loss of my horse.”

“Please don’t make a rushed decision. Remember, your dad wanted you to have that house. And Colton is a good guy.” Rayna reached across the small table and squeezed Trisha’s hand.

“I’ll remember. I promise.”

“Good. Ready for another drink?” Rayna asked.

“Sure.” Trisha glanced around for their waitress. At least she’d made one decision. She’d spend some time up north and see how she felt in a few days.

* * *

It was dark by the time Colton pulled into his driveway. He’d spent most of the day at the track, then, on a whim, drove out to the lake. Immersed in contemplation by the water's edge, he lost track of time until the sun had long dipped below the horizon.

As he maneuvered into his driveway, his headlights shone on a big fluffy cat sitting on his front porch. Stepping out of his truck, he approached the feline. The cat brushed against his denim-clad leg as it emitted a pitiful meow.

"Hey there, where'd you come from?" Colton reached down to pat its furry head. He received another meow in response, as the kitty walked between his legs. Glancing around and not spotting anyone searching for their missing pet, Colton decided to open the door. The second he did, without hesitation, the cat darted inside.

"Okay, come on in before a hungry coyote gets you."

Inside, Colton headed to the fridge, grabbed himself a cold long neck, then poured some milk into a saucer and presented it to the cat. Afterward, he strolled outside, stood under the porchlight, and sipped his beer.

About five minutes later, a blonde in tight shorts and a white T-shirt emerged from the side of his house. Noticing him, she inquired, "Have you seen Mr. Cuddles?"

He lifted his eyebrows and started to ask her to repeat the question.

"I'm sorry, I mean my cat. He ran out of the house, and I can't find him."

"You found him. He's inside."

"Oh, thank goodness. I've been so worried. I just moved in. I had the door open while hauling some boxes inside and he ran out."

"Come on in and get him."

"Thank you. I'm Mandy, by the way. Your new neighbor." She stepped onto the porch and held out her hand.

"Colton. Pleased to meet you." He accepted her offered hand and gave it a gentle shake. Opening the door, he gestured for her to enter.

* * *

I can't just send Colton a breakup text.

Trisha knew she'd be furious if he pulled that on her. So, leaving the bar and heading home, she made a spontaneous decision to swing by Colton's. She'd explain to him in person the reasons for taking some alone time. How she needed to think about what she really wanted in life. He'd understand.

Yet, as she approached, she saw him and a blonde woman entering his house.

What the—

Suspicion set in, he had company, seemingly indifferent to her text message. Then it dawned on her. Colton probably hadn't even seen the text, engrossed as he was entertaining someone else. A wave of sickness washed over her as she witnessed him closing the front door behind them.

How could he do this? she screamed internally. Tears now stinging her eyes, she stepped hard on the gas, the tires squealing as she sped away.

Chapter Thirty

For the next three weeks, Trisha engaged in a period of doing next to nothing. She'd packed a few personal items and clothing, then headed north to her dad's property. She was still struggling with the belief it belonged to her and clinging to the hope that immersing herself in a daily routine there would weave a sense of belonging and familiarity into her consciousness. And ease the pain of losing Icy Tears.

"I haven't eaten this well since I still lived at home with my mom. This was delicious," Trisha said to Martha as she placed her fork down and picked up her napkin.

A faint blush graced Martha's cheeks in response to the compliment. They were seated on the screened-in back porch of Trisha's new home, the area that stretched the entire length of the house. Green plants adorned the floor in large pots, and blooming flowers hung from the ceiling in baskets. The glass-topped table where they ate offered a perfect view of the pasture where Colton's horse and Charlie's were grazing. Trisha certainly couldn't deny the beauty of the place.

"I can see why my dad loved it up here so much. It's beautiful." Trisha savored another sip of her mimosa.

"Oh, your daddy sure did enjoy himself when he was here. We had some good times." Martha chuckled, white curls bouncing across her shoulders. "We'd have BBQs for the neighbors. Everyone came. Charlie smoked meat for days." A nostalgic sigh escaped her lips. "And the stories your daddy could tell us about the racetrack." She lowered her voice with a conspiratorial tone, "I think he made most of them up." Another bout of laughter followed.

"Those times must have been wonderful," Trisha mused aloud, her thoughts drifting to the tale about the lively gatherings of the past. "I wish I'd have been here." She turned her gaze toward the grazing horses, imagining the stories and laughter that had filled the air.

Martha rose from her seat, beginning to collect some of the plates. "I'm going to clean everything up. You sit right where you are and let me do it. Then I've got to get home and put a cake in the oven. I promised my carrot cake for the church bake sale this weekend."

Martha's efficiency and commitment to her community activities were evident, and Trisha nodded appreciatively, settling back to enjoy the view while Martha took care of the post-meal tasks.

Trisha lingered in the sunroom for another fifteen minutes, captivated by the horses still grazing in the pasture while reflecting on her life. The roller coaster of emotions was undeniable, especially when it came to Colton. A yearning for a different outcome with him persisted. She missed their conversations, their shared laughter, and the intimacy she'd believed they had. Regrettably, it seemed she had misinterpreted his feelings. And after this long of not hearing from him, well, she got the picture. She didn't have a horse for him to train, so he didn't need her in his life.

I don't need him either.

Taking a soothing breath, she stood, strolled into the kitchen, and poured herself a cup of coffee. Then, cradling the mug, she meandered into the front room, deciding it was high time to check her neglected emails. As far as she could recall, three days had passed since her last check, a testament to her turbulent state of mind. She couldn't seem to focus on anything lately, she was so depressed. Her once-promising racing business was stagnant; people she trusted broke her heart, and she wasn't sure what to do next.

As her computer hummed to life, a sound from outside caught her attention. Moving to the window, she peered out to see a livestock van had pulled into her driveway.

Intrigued, she made her way to the front door.

Stepping out of the house and onto the front porch, Trisha gasped. It was Colton climbing out of the rig. He glanced over and offered a friendly wave as he walked to the rear doors.

What the bloody Hell?

What was he doing here, and what the heck did he have with him? Curiosity piqued, Trisha trailed him around to the side of the van and watched him drop the ramp.

"Go ahead. Have a look." He stepped back slightly, giving her plenty of room.

She stared at him, confused but interested. She peeked inside. A horse appeared to be sleeping. His eyes were half closed, his big head drooping down, almost hitting his chest.

"Don't worry, it's just a light tranquilizer to keep him calm for the ride. He'll wake up soon."

"Oh, my God, Colton. Is this who I think it is?" Tears threatened to spill over her cheeks. "Icy? It's Icy Tears. How...how did you manage?"

Colton chuckled. "It's a long story. But he's all yours now." Colton jumped inside the van and, after a minute, emerged with an unsteady Thoroughbred in tow.

* * *

Colton watched Icy Tears amble over to the feed trough and grab a sample of fresh hay. As the horse chewed lazily, he turned to Trisha, "he'll be fine."

"I can't believe he's here." Her eyes shimmered as if she was about to cry.

"I promised you I'd make things right." Colton gently traced his finger along her cheek, but she swatted his hand away.

"What's the matter?" he inquired, suddenly confused.

"Nothing," She replied, brushing hay from her jeans. She stepped closer to the stall and her gaze focused on Icy Tears as he munched the hay.

"Have I done something wrong? I thought you wanted your horse."

"Absolutely, I want Icy Tears. Thank you for bringing him here." Her back was still turned to him.

He took a step closer and started to touch her shoulder, then hesitated, sensing the tension in the air. "Do you want to talk about it?"

She turned to face him. "There's nothing to talk about, Colton. You made your feelings clear over the past weeks by not calling me." Her tone carried a mix of hurt and frustration.

"Your text said you needed time to sort things out. I was respecting your wishes."

"I'm sure you were, and I appreciate that, but it didn't take long for you to move on," she accused, bitterness laced her words.

"Move on?" He scratched the back of his neck. "I don't follow—"

"Colton," she interrupted. "You had a date the night you received that text. I know because I felt bad about sending it, so I drove to your house. Just in time to see you and a blonde walking inside." She put her hand on her hips and snapped, "I hope you had a nice evening."

"Blonde? I didn't date a blonde. I didn't date anyone."

"I saw you with my own two eyes. Don't try to deny it."

He sucked in a deep breath while trying to replay that night in his mind. Then he remembered. "Wait a minute. That was my new neighbor. She came by to get Cuddles."

"Well, that makes it just fine. Only for cuddles."

"No. I mean Mr. Cuddles. Her cat. He was lost. I found him and kept him until she picked him up. There was no date. She didn't stay more than five minutes. Just grabbed her cat and left."

"Oh." Trisha's eyes narrowed thoughtfully. Her bottom lip trembled slightly. After a second, embarrassment colored her cheeks as she lifted her shoulders in a shrug. "Well...I guess I jumped to the wrong conclusion."

Colton pulled her close. "It doesn't matter anymore. We're together and I'm not letting you get away." He folded her into his arms and realized she was trembling. "Trisha. I promise I'll never hurt you." He kissed the top of her head.

"God, I'm such a bitch." Tears trailed along her cheeks. "I'm really sorry."

He took her chin in his hand and raised her head, so their eyes met. "I love you, honey," he whispered as he wiped her tears away with his thumb.

"I love you too. Since the first day we met."

"Let's go to the house," he whispered as he scooped her up and then kissed her passionately.

Completely caught up in the moment, he wasn't watching where he walked. He'd just carried her outside the double doors of the barn when he tripped on a garden hose catapulting them both to the ground. They were both laughing hysterically as they ended up covered in grass and leaves.

"I feel like we've done this before," Trisha teased as she kissed him again.

Before Colton had a chance to reply, she pulled herself off him and held out her hand. He stood, took her hand, and softly squeezed, letting the warmth of her fingers flow into his.

They stopped at the passenger side of the truck and grabbed his bags, then both still smiling, they headed toward the house.

"I need you so much, Trisha," he whispered as he reached the front porch steps.

"I need you most," she answered as she opened the door.

Chapter Thirty-One

Still holding his hand, Trisha led Colton straight to her bedroom. No words were spoken as they entered the room and gazed into each other's eyes. Lifting her hand to the front of Colton's shirt, she unbuttoned and slid it off his broad shoulders. Leaning forward, she kissed his bare chest, then closed her eyes, and inhaled his scent as she enjoyed the luxurious feeling of his fingers rubbing up and down the back of her neck.

A soft moan escaped from deep in her throat as his hands moved down, slid under her sweater, and gently lifted it over her head. Her skin quivered as his fingers unhooked her bra and pushed it off her shoulders. As the cool air in the bedroom fanned across her nipples, they both turned to stiff peaks, begging to be touched. Colton's lips and teeth obeyed as he began to toy with first one, then the other, until Trisha thought she'd go crazy with need.

His hands continued to stroke her heated skin as she removed her remaining clothing.

"I'm a mess. I need a shower."

"I can't wait that long." Suddenly, his arms circled around her, and he lifted, spinning her toward the bed in one swift movement. They landed on the soft mattress, his body pressing against hers.

"It's been a long time, honey," he whispered near her ear. His warm breath sent more shivers through her body.

"I know," she answered. "I thought we'd never be like this again. I'm so glad I was wrong."

He lifted himself off her, stood next to the bed, and quickly disrobed as she watched with hungry eyes. Then he moved over her, pressing his body to hers. He felt so good, so strong. "I want you so much," she told him as he parted her legs with one of his own. "So much."

"Wrap your legs around me," he suggested. As he'd directed, she curled her legs over his.

"Yeah, baby, just like that." He pushed himself inside her, joining their bodies as one. Their tongues danced together as she lifted her hips trying to pull him deeper into her. Heat rose between them as he plunged inside her again and again until they came together in a surge of adrenaline and need.

Afterward, they lay quiet, just holding each other. As Trisha's breathing returned to normal, she opened her eyes to find Colton staring at her. She blushed. "Am I a mess?"

"You're beautiful."

He ran his finger through her hair as he spoke bringing a slight smile to her lips. She looked into his eyes and slowly brought her hand to his cheek. "So, now will you tell me how you showed up today with my horse?"

He rolled over and onto his elbow and rested his head in his hand. "Tell you what, baby. Let's take a nice hot shower, then raid the fridge, and while we eat, I'll fill you in with the entire story."

"You got a deal." She scooted off the bed, grabbed her robe, and raced him to the bathroom.

* * *

Colton rummaged through the refrigerator while Trisha checked the kitchen cabinets. "Don't you buy food?" he asked when he realized there wasn't much to choose from besides some wilted lettuce and a carton of eggs.

"I haven't had to. Martha keeps showing up with my meals."

He shrugged. "I suppose we can scramble some eggs. Do you have bread for toast?"

"Hey, I just remembered, there's lasagna in the freezer. How do you feel about Italian?"

"Right now, I'd eat the pan it's in too."

"Great. I'll start heating it up." Trisha said, her enthusiasm evident as she moved toward the freezer.

"While you do that, I'm going to check Icy Tears. I'll feel better knowing he's fully awake and settled in."

"Okay. I'll see you in a few."

By the time he returned to the kitchen, the warm glow of candles flickered, casting a soft ambiance over the room. "Well, this is nice," he admitted, a hint of surprise in his voice as he took in the unexpected effort she had put into the setting.

"Just because it's leftovers doesn't mean we can't enjoy a nice evening." She pointed toward the counter. "Will you pour the wine while I dish up our meal?"

Colton filled the glasses to almost overflowing and inhaled the lasagna as he set their glasses on the table. His mouth began to water. "Looks delicious."

"Sit and enjoy," Trisha instructed, pointing to a chair.

They ate their food slowly while exchanging glances over their wine glasses. Finally, Colton figured she'd waited long enough to hear the details of his past weeks. "Ready to hear how I got Icy Tears?"

Trisha's eyes sparkled with curiosity. "I'm dying to know," she replied, her fork pausing mid-air as she waited for the story to unfold. The soft glow of the candles seemed to intensify, adding a touch of suspense to the cozy scene as they prepared to share more than just a meal.

He took a deep breath and began, "After you left for the clubhouse, I paid Ledger a visit. I offered to buy Icy Tears back. I told him I'd return his claim money. He laughed. So, I asked him what his price was."

"And?" She leaned forward.

"Fifty thousand dollars."

"Say what! That's ridiculous. He's a great horse, but certainly that amount's absurd."

"That's what I said. So, Ledger gave me a better option."

"Well, thank goodness."

"Forty-five thousand dollars, and I could have him."

"That's better? Good grief, Colton." Her eyes widened then she blinked. "So, I don't understand. How could you afford that price?"

"I had to get creative. First, I sold Patty's Red Royal for her owner and got my commission, then I sold Moonlit Mirage."

"Oh, no. You didn't. Colton, not Moonlit Mirage?"

"Yeah, got a decent price for her too. Of course, I was still a long way from the money I needed. So, I took a loan out of my truck."

"And that was enough?"

"Nope. Not anywhere close."

"So? Then what?"

"I learned that Ledger had entered both horses, Tribal Jack and Icy Tears in a sixty-thousand stakes race."

He met Trisha's stare, smiling at her deer-in-the-headlights appearance.

"Honey, I saw only one thing to do."

"You didn't?" Her hand covered her heart, the suspense and concern evident in her still wide-eyed expression.

"I did. I went all or nothing. I bet my entire bankroll on those two horses. And believe it or not, they came in exactly as I had bet." A rush of emotions swept through Colton—the tension of the gamble, the relief of victory, and the vulnerability of sharing his journey all laid bare in that moment.

Trisha's eyes mirrored the rollercoaster, and for a heartbeat, the room seemed to hold the echoes of a risky decision turned triumphant.

"That's crazy. You could have lost everything. Then what? Then you have nothing."

"It definitely could have gone the other way," he admitted. "But I'd run out of options to get the money and I had to get your horse back. I made you a promise."

"You could have come to me. I would have given you the money."

"Nope," Couldn't do that. I'm the one who talked you into running in a claiming race and lost him...and lost you." He shrugged, then remained silent, waiting for her to respond.

Trisha finally spoke. "I can't have a relationship with a gambler." She eyed him closely. "I realize horse racing is a risk but foolish gambling…I just can't." She leaned forward, cupping his face in her hand. "Can you promise me you'll never do anything so reckless again?"

"That's an easy promise. Watching that race almost gave me a heart attack. Besides, being that lucky twice could never happen in a million years."

Her eyebrows raised. "You are one crazy dude."

"Yeah, but you love me, right?"

Chapter Thirty-Two

The following months were filled with Trisha learning more about horses, having fun, and lots and lots of sex.

Home sweet home.

Trisha glanced around at the property left to her by her dad and smiled. She couldn't be happier. With an exaggerated exhale, Trisha hoisted the final box from the bed of Colton's truck. Alongside her friends, Scarlett, and Rayna, she had coordinated the transition of her belongings from her condo to her new home, leaving behind most of the furniture for the incoming tenant.

As luck would have it, Rayna needed to move, so the condo would become her residence, allowing Trisha to make the new house a full-time arrangement with Colton. And with a work-from-home agreement in place, Trisha would be required only to make a once-a-month excursion to Phoenix for meetings. So far, every piece of this puzzle was seamlessly falling into place.

"Well, that's the last of it. I think we're finally finished." Trisha gently set the heavy box down on the front porch, then wiped her sweaty hands on her worn-out jeans.

"You're so lucky to live here," Scarlett exclaimed. "It's beautiful, and the summers will be much cooler than Phoenix."

"That's *definitely* a big plus. Just make sure you keep a room available for us," Rayna chimed in.

"You know I will. And I expect you both to visit at least once a month," Trisha said, the realization suddenly hitting that she wouldn't be seeing her friends as often. She blinked back tears, determined not to let them fall.

"Group hug," Trisha exclaimed, enfolding her friends in a tight embrace. As they hugged, she caught sight of Colton walking toward them, curiosity etched across his face.

"What's going on, ladies?" he asked as he reached their huddle.

Breaking free from their embrace, Trisha reached for his hand. "Hey, honey, we've brought the last of my things."

"Great. Come on out to the barn. I'll show you how we've progressed." His face lit into a proud smile reflecting the hard work he'd put into his carpentry.

"Colton and Charlie are building more stalls. We want to add more horses," Trisha explained to Scarlett and Rayna, a hint of excitement in her voice. "Let's see how they're doing."

"Sure." Scarlett and Rayna fell in behind Trisha and Colton as they headed toward the barn.

Entering, the atmosphere transformed as the scent of fresh hay, animals, leather, and the additional smell of sawed lumber enveloped them. Charlie, perspiring and focused, adjusted the door to the newly constructed stall. He turned to them, wiping his hand across his brow. "Well, this is the last one. Now you've got room for more horses," he said, starting to gather his tools.

"Looks wonderful," Trisha replied, taking a deep breath to savor the mixture of scents she had come to love. Then, scanning the surroundings, she inquired, "Where's Icy Tears? And Maverick and Lucky?"

"Take a look." Colton smiled and he pointed to the open barn doors.

Leaving Charlie to finish up his work they headed outside. Walking slowly to the fence they all gazed toward the paddock. Immediately, Lucky raised his head and nickered. Maverick was toward the back corner under the shade of a tree grazing and seemed unfazed as the four people lined up against the white rails.

"I don't see Icy Tears." Trisha shaded her eyes with one hand to help her block to sunshine.

"Over to your far left. Here he comes." Colton pointed to the north side of the paddock.

All eyes turned as Icy Tears came into view. At the sight of them, the big horse lifted his tail and bolted, running the length of the paddock, dark mane flying. He was a living, breathing embodiment of beauty and power. He reached the far end, stopped, snorted, then took off again.

"He's showing off for you ladies now." Colton laughed.

Smiling, Trisha stepped closer to Colton and leaned her head against his broad shoulder. "He looks happy, doesn't he?"

"I say he does," Colton replied. Then, putting his hand on her waist, he pulled her close and asked, "How about you? Are you happy?"

Trisha gazed into his eyes, then turned back to watch Icy Tears. He was still at the far end of the paddock but had stopped running. He lifted his proud head, snorted loudly then pawed the ground with one foreleg. "Colton, remember when you told me this life gets into your blood?"

"I remember."

"You were right. I love it here." She brushed at a tear that attempted to trail down her cheek. "This is where I belong."

"It's a good life, Trisha." His blue eyes locked on hers as he added, "the one your daddy wanted for you."

"I wish I could tell him thank you."

"He knows, honey. He knows."

Trisha's bottom lip trembled as she tried to smile.

"Hey," Rayna interjected, "isn't it about cocktail hour?"

"I'm thinking it is," Scarlett added. "That is, if the two love birds can break apart long enough to join us."

Trisha looked at Colton and shrugged. Then, turning to her friends, she instructed, "One of you better go make some margaritas."

Chapter Thirty-Three

The arrival of summer was swift. After buying Icy Tears back from Ledger, Colton invested the remaining funds by purchasing two more decent horses. He and Charlie had started working with them daily. Bree drove up on weekends and helped with the workouts, giving Charlie a break. All in all, they felt they had a good chance of bringing in some future money. As far as Icy Tears racing again, that would be Trisha's decision.

Colton leaned against the stall wall as Charlie led a horse in and stuffed hay into the net. He glanced at his hands, sore and calloused from all the construction work he had done in the barn. He hadn't manually worked this hard in years, but it felt good. Inwardly, he smiled.

"This one's good for today." Charlie exited the stall and scribbled something on his clipboard.

"Good job," Colton praised the older man. He'd been an enormous help lately, and he knew he couldn't have accomplished nearly as much without him. "I was thinking about taking a day off this weekend. If you can manage around here without me,"

Charlie grinned, the lines on his face telling tales of years working outside dealing with the demands of horses. "I've spent a lot of time managing by myself. Besides, Bree will be here to exercise the horses. You go do what you need to. And I'd say it was about time." He winked, moving toward the next stall where a new horse greeted him with a nicker.

Colton ran his hand over the back of his neck, then whistling an old country tune, picked up a water bucket.

The weekend rolled around, and he asked Trisha if she wanted to take an evening drive. He tried to act casually. Then, as she turned to grab a sweater, he slipped a small package into his jacket pocket. An hour and a half later, they pulled into the parking lot of the expansive lake.

Colton parked the truck, and together, they strolled to the boardwalk. As they did, the desert air carried the scent of sunbaked earth, mingling with the tangy aroma of a lakeside BBQ restaurant. A breeze blew across the water, sending ripples in its wake.

"It's lovely out here at night," Trisha remarked.

"Sure is," Colton replied as he inhaled a deep breath. Wow, she was beautiful. She'd curled her hair, and it hung in waves cascading over her shoulders just the way he liked. He fought the urge to run his fingers through it. Clearing his throat, he spoke, "I have a little surprise. A friend of mine loaned us his boat for tonight." He arched his eyebrows and asked, "How do you feel about a midnight cruise?"

"Well, I'm game, but it's not midnight."

"It's dark, so good enough."

She smiled, then frowned as she asked, "You can drive a boat?"

"Used to boat here a lot." He shrugged. "Years ago."

"My man of many talents."

"Yeah, that's me."

Colton led her to where several boats were lined up at the dock, their hulls gently rocking with the ebb and flow of the breeze-rippled water. The distant sounds of laughter and music from the nearby restaurant added to the lively atmosphere.

Before long, they found themselves aboard the borrowed boat, the gentle creaking of the dock giving way to the subtle hum of the engine as he skillfully navigated them onto the deserted lake. Overhead, the stars twinkled in a cosmic dance, and the full moon was climbing into the night sky, casting its ethereal glow across the water.

The moonlight turned the waves into a mesmerizing display of silver ripples, creating a shimmering image stretching out to the horizon. He guided the boat with a steady hand, the breeze tousling their hair as they moved into the open expanse of water.

A person couldn't help but be captivated by the moment's beauty, Colton mused. The cool night air, the reflection of stars on the water, and the boat's speed created a surreal atmosphere. It was a scene that evoked a sense of freedom and exhilaration. Still, he couldn't contain a nervous grin, hoping Trisha shared the thrill of this impromptu adventure as much as he did.

"I never know what to expect from you."

He chuckled anxiously to himself, knowing he had one more surprise planned.

When they reached a small bay area, Colton slowed the boat and turned to Trisha. "Do you like it here?"

She glanced around and answered in a breathless whisper, "It seems magical."

With a quiet determination, he killed the engine and dropped the anchor. Sliding onto the seat beside her, he noticed her shiver and, without a word, wrapped an arm around her shoulders. "Are you cold?"

She hesitated for a moment before replying, "Not really. I'm fine."

"Good. I thought we'd sit here a little while and talk."

"Okay. What do you want to talk about?"

"About us. Trisha." He took her hand in his and cleared his throat. He decided to come right out and ask her before losing his nerve. "I love you. Marry me. Let's build a life together." He produced a small black velvet box from his pocket and held it toward her.

"Colton, I—"

"I know. I don't have much to offer you. Not now anyway, but I will."

"No." She put her other hand over his. "That's not a problem, it's just so sudden."

"So, you don't want to get married?" He felt his heart sink.

"No, I do. I mean, yes," she reassured him, a genuine smile spread across her face.

"You do? You mean it?"

"I mean it. Yes, Colton McKenna, I'll marry you." She took the box and opened it. Inside was a white gold ring with a stunning marquis stone surrounded by smaller diamonds. She let out a soft gasp.

"Here, let me." He removed the ring and slipped it on her trembling finger. "I hope you like it."

"Oh, Colton, I love it." She held up her hand and wiggled her finger, letting the diamond sparkle under the moonlight.

"I should have brought champagne."

"Or the whiskey bottle you used to have stashed in your truck."

"I'm slipping in the romance department."

She held up her hand again and smiled. "You're doing just fine."

Colton didn't know what their future held. Would he keep training racehorses or start the breeding stable he'd envisioned lately? All he knew was that the possibilities were endless with Trisha by his side.

"I love you." He grabbed her and kissed her passionately. Breaking their kiss, he promised, "I'll give you a good life, Trisha." Then, pulling her against his chest, he added, "And you know I'm a man of my word."

Chapter Thirty-Four

Spring in the high desert is a delightful blend of crisp air, carrying the refreshing scent of ponderosa pines and junipers and an earthy aroma of awaking wildflowers. The afternoons are warm, but a pleasant coolness lingers from the early mornings. The sky stretching overhead is a brilliant blue canvas, occasionally adorned with fluffy white clouds drifting lazily across the horizon. It perfectly balances vibrant colors and a restoring sense of new beginnings. And the ideal setting for a wedding.

It had been eight months since Colton proposed to Trisha, and the excitement of the wedding day was in full swing. They had decided on an outside wedding to be held at their home with just family and a few close friends attending. Charlie would smoke a brisket and a turkey and put some ribs on the barbecue. The rest of the menu was to be catered. A local bakery would deliver their wedding cake, and Martha would ensure it arrived on time.

"Hold still," Scarlett instructed Trisha with a gentle laugh. "We wouldn't want champagne stains on this gorgeous dress of yours." Scarlett meticulously poured champagne into the flute Trisha held.

"Sorry," Trisha apologized, her nerves evident. Her dress was as she'd always imagined her wedding gown would look. A lovely ivory satin strapless with pearls across the bodice. The back featured an alluring corset closure, allowing a customized fit and an added element of romance. She took a calming breath and gazed into the mirror on her bedroom wall.

Rayna, consulting a list they had crafted during the initial stages of planning, chimed in, "Your dress is new, the veil from Rebecca is borrowed, and blue...what's blue?"

"Her sapphire earrings," Scarlett replied, deftly adjusting the pearl-trimmed veil into Trisha's hairstyle.

"Where *is* Rebecca?" Trisha asked before taking a generous sip of the champagne. "I hope she's not running late. Traffic can get backed up."

"I saw her drive in with Mick. The guys in his band were right behind them. She's probably with him while they're getting set up. Don't worry." Scarlett assured her.

"I can't help it. Oh," she gasped, "what if it rains?"

"I've checked the weather. It will be perfect." Rayna placed the list on the dresser. "Trisha needs something old. What do we have that's old?"

A soft rapping on the door interrupted them. Rayna ran over and cracked it slightly open, making sure it wasn't Colton trying to peek in on his bride.

"Hi," a woman softly spoke.

"Mom." Trisha beamed, handed Scarlett her champagne, and crossed the room in a heartbeat. "Come in." Embracing her mother warmly, a cascade of emotions surged through her. Tears welled in her eyes as she held her mother tightly. "I was hoping you'd make it."

"Of course. I couldn't miss my little girl's wedding." The words carried the weight of missed moments and a longing for connection. Her eyes brimmed with tears as her arms tightened around her daughter. "I'm so sorry, Trisha. I should never have kept your father from you. It was wrong and selfish of me. Just because I couldn't understand his lifestyle doesn't mean I had the right to judge him for you."

At that moment, the months of physical distance evaporated. "It's okay, Mom. We all do things we wish we could change."

"I brought you something." Her mother reached into her purse and produced an old photograph. "This was taken on our wedding day. See how handsome your dad was in his suit." She handed the photo to Trisha. "I thought you might like to tuck it in your bouquet."

"Oh, Mom." Trisha's eyes shimmered with happiness as she tightly embraced her mother. "This is absolutely perfect."

"Let's get your mom some champagne," Rayna suggested.

A few minutes later, the four of them were enjoying a happy toast when Rebecca walked in. "Look at you all partying without me," she teased as she walked over and hugged Trisha.

"Right, here is your glass." Scarlett handed Rebecca a champagne-filled flute, seamlessly integrating her into the festivities.

"Thanks," Rebecca replied before shifting the focus to the impending ceremony. After a sip of champagne, she informed Trisha that the band was set up and ready to start.

At that moment, Martha stepped in and announced, "It's time, Trisha."

"Let me go get seated." Trisha's mother hugged her tightly. "You look beautiful, darling." She kissed her daughter quickly and then hurried out of the bedroom to find her seat as the bride's mother.

"All right now, girls, go find your places," Martha declared with a clap of her hands. "Trisha, Charlie's waiting to walk you down the aisle."

"Almost ready," Trisha blotted her eyes, making sure no tears had ruined her make-up. Then she picked up the photo of her dad and carefully tucked it into her bouquet, securely wedging it between the yellow roses and Gerber daisies. "Now," she took a calming breath. "Let's go." Grabbing Martha's outstretched hand, they headed outside.

Standing on the patio, watching her three best friends slowly walk down the aisle between the chairs on the lawn, her heart swelled with love. Tears of happiness formed when Rebecca, Scarlett, and Rayna, dressed in sage green dresses, took their place at the rose-covered arch. Next, Colton walked to his spot, looking handsome in his custom-tailored charcoal grey suit and spit-shined cowboy boots. Equally sharp, dressed in matching tailored vests, the groomsmen, José and B.J., stepped to the altar and lined up beside him.

How did I get so lucky? It seems like only yesterday I was searching everywhere for someone to fill the void in my heart. All I had to do was open my eyes and see who was right before me.

"You ready, honey?" Charlie asked, bringing her thoughts back to the present.

A soft breeze caressed her bare shoulders. In the distance, a horse whinnied, and she felt her father's presence surrounding her. There was no doubt in her mind that he was watching over her and smiling with approval.

"I've never been so ready," she whispered. Gripping Charlie's strong arm, Trisha inhaled deeply and took the first step toward her new life.

Epilogue

One year later.
    Trisha stood on the front porch of her newly renovated home and watched Colton pull the horse van up the gravel driveway. Her heart raced excitedly as he slowed to a gentle stop near the barn. When she caught Colton's attention, he waved and hopped out of the driver's side as she hurried to meet him.

    "I've missed you," she wrapped her arms around his neck and kissed him hard.

    "I've missed you too, Baby. Wait till you see what I brought home," he replied with a mischievous twinkle in his eyes.

    Trisha's curiosity piqued, she looked at him expectantly. "What have you done?"

    Colton gestured towards the van. Then, moving her toward the back, he lifted the latch. As the rear door was pulled open, the movement of hooves on the metal flooring became audible. "Happy Anniversary."

    Trisha's eyes widened with delight as she caught sight of two horses—one grey and one almost black.

"Oh, what a wonderful surprise. I had no idea."

At that moment, Charlie ran out of the barn. "What's going on?"

"Charlie, come get these horses unloaded. Let Trisha have a look at them."

"Hey, you got them both. Good job." He patted Colton on the shoulder.

"Charlie, you knew about this?" Trisha questioned.

"Sure. Your husband called and told me to have a couple of stalls ready."

"Oh, you two." Her hand covered her mouth, and she shook her head, laughing.

"Get the grey horse out of the van first."

Charlie walked up the ramp and into the van, disappearing briefly from Trisha's view. After a moment, he reappeared, leading a grey filly carefully down the short ramp and onto the lush grass surrounding the barn.

"Colton, she's beautiful. She reminds me of the horse I saw in the liquidation sale catalog. The one with the pretty face."

"The one and same. I found her at an auction in Del Mar. When I saw her, I knew you'd want her."

Trisha couldn't contain the excitement within her, and her breath caught as she focused on the newest addition to Victory Lane Stable. The filly's sleek grey coat glistened in the sunlight, and every step she took seemed to exude grace and strength.

Charlie, with a proud smile, guided the Thoroughbred closer. As Trisha stood mesmerized, he turned the horse around. Her dark eyes gleamed with intelligence, her nostrils flared with a mixture of curiosity and anticipation.

Stepping nearer, Trisha ran her hand gently along the grey's neck, feeling the smoothness of her coat beneath her fingertips. The horse nuzzled her affectionately, forging an instant connection between them.

"She's magnificent," Trisha whispered in awe. "What's her name?"

Colton grinned and nodded. "Meet Luna Serenade."

Trisha smiled happily as she watched Charlie walk Luna Serenade to the paddock. Then, after turning her loose, he secured the gate.

He quickly returned to the van and came back out, grinning, leading the black mare. When all four feet were on the ground, she lifted her ebony head high and looked around wide-eyed at the strange surroundings.

"She's beautiful, too," Trisha reached up to gently stroke the mare's velvet nose. "Hello, pretty lady. It's okay," she spoke calmly. "You're going to love it here." The mare snorted and flicked her ears.

"I knew you'd like her." Colton stepped next to her. "And she's in foal. She's your first broodmare."

Meeting his gaze, she replied, "I'm overwhelmed."

"She's got good breeding and carries the foal of a champion. She's just right for our growing stable."

Trisha nodded in reply, her eyes still fixed on Colton. At that moment, as she stood surrounded by the beauty of the horses, the barn, and the sprawling green pastures, Trisha knew that the dream she and Colton had was not only coming to fruition but was surpassing their wildest expectations. She still had Icy Tears, and now Luna Serenade and this beautiful black mare, and soon she'd have a new foal.

Life was good.

"Go ahead and take this one to a stall, get her settled and fed," Colton instructed Charlie. "Then bring in the filly. I'll check back after a while." Smiling, Colton draped his arm over Trisha's shoulder and headed toward the house.

Sometime later, as they lay in bed basking in the afterglow of heated lovemaking, Trisha rested her head against Colton's chest. As he stroked her hair, she said softly, "You really are amazing."

"You're the amazing one. You look prettier today than when I left four days ago." He slid his fingers along her bare shoulders. "I got some news you'll find interesting."

She lifted her head. "You do? So, spill it."

He chuckled. "Guess who got busted for drugging his horses?"

"No. I'm hoping Ledger?"

"You guessed correctly. His trainer admitted it was Ledger who insisted they use drugs."

"What happens to him now?"

"Probably not as much as we'd like. He'll get fined. It'll keep him from running horses the rest of the meet and put a black mark on his name."

"I guess that's a start."

"It is. The track stewards will keep a close eye on him and whoever he hires as a trainer. It'll make it harder for him to get away with his shenanigans."

"It's about time."

"Forget Ledger." He pulled her on top of him, lifting her up so he could let his fingers glide across her firm, generous breasts.

"Forgotten," she whispered as she leaned forward and began to run her tongue slowly along his neck.

A moan escaped his throat as she continued her trail of kisses down, then up again, until her lips were close to his ear. "I love you, Colton."

"I love you."

Trisha felt his arousal begin again. She tilted her head, letting her dark mass of hair fall over her face to seductively caress his shoulder. Her gaze traveled downward to notice how his body was reacting to her.

He raised an eyebrow in question.

"Again," she purred as she wrapped her hand around his ramrod-straight erection.

"Again," he agreed, pulling her into his arms.

Hours later, Trisha and Colton cuddled on the couch, munching freshly baked pizza and sipping ice-cold beer. The only sound in the room was the cracking of the fireplace and the soft strum of Charlie's guitar wafting in from the front porch of the nearby guest house. Charlie's melodic guitar chords provided a serene soundtrack, adding an extra layer of harmony to the evening.

Time seemed to slow down as they savored each bite, each sip, and each note, relishing the simple pleasures that made this shared experience so special.

Finished with her food, Trisha leaned her head on Colton's shoulder and began reflecting on bygone days. She reminisced about the times she and her girlfriends had tirelessly scoured local bars in pursuit of the ideal companion. Those weekends seemed a distant memory now.

Lifting her head, she glanced up at Colton, wondering how her life would have unfolded had her father not bequeathed his legacy, intertwining their fates. The thought filled her with gratitude, unable to fathom a more fulfilling life than the one she shared with this man who held her heart.

Colton glanced toward her. "Everything okay?"

A soft smile graced her lips as she replied, "Everything's perfect."

And indeed, it was.

The End

Dani Petrone is a multi-published author who divides her writing time between her own stories to being half of the Books We Love award-winning team Tia Dani.

Dani resides in Arizona with her fourteen-year-old cat and a senior one-eyed dog. When not writing, you might find her drinking butterscotch martinis with her author friends, playing on social media, or binge-watching suspense movies. She also enjoys touring luxury homes, exploring haunted hot spots, and taking scenic road trips.

Dani's an active member of several writing groups, including a member of The Butterscotch Martini Girls.